AMAZON REVIEWS
JACKSON BL

Kept my interest enough to read 3 books in a day.

I can't say enough about the Jackson Blackhawk series! Fast moving with exciting plots that keep the reader engaged. Buy them. Read them You'll be glad you found this series.

Run—do not walk—to buy this book! (The Girl at the Deep End of the Lake).

I couldn't put this book down!

Wonderfully developed colorful characters without going overboard with super hero powers.

This is a very good read, I like this kind of story and the way it is written makes all the difference to me, this writer has done a great job.

They Called Her Indigo

SAM LEE JACKSON

Piping Rock Publications
3608 E Taro Lane. Phoenix AZ 85050
www.samleejackson.com

ISBN: 978-0-9998526-7-5
Library of Congress Control Number: 2018959212

For CJ. My rock, my partner, my muse, my lover,
my companion, my teacher and my all.

ACKNOWLEDGMENTS

Thanks to my talented and painstaking editor, Ann Hedrick. My amazing cover illustrator, Mariah Sinclair, and my website guru Lance Robinson. And of course, my readers who make all things possible.

1

The girl was white blonde, her hair in a short cut that swept across her forehead. She was quite beautiful in a young pixie kind of way. She was very good. She waited until my machine hit, then when she put her hands into my clothes I didn't feel a thing. But, I knew she did it. The only thing I noticeably felt was the absence of weight of my wallet as she turned to move away. I waited a moment before I glanced at her. I swiveled on my stool and looked the other way at Blackhawk. He was three slot machines down watching, a smile on his face. I shrugged, cashed out of the machine, pulled my card and slid off my stool. He followed suit.

He went the long way around two lines of slot machines, all the while keeping her in sight. I followed more directly, staying well back. She didn't target any more guys, but wound through the crowd to the back, where a bank of elevators awaited.

We were at one of the Indian tribe casinos that populate the Phoenix area. I never could figure out the law that said Native Americans could own gambling establishments, but other races couldn't. I'm sure there was some kind of reason, but since I don't gamble, it wasn't something I stayed up nights worrying about. Besides, Blackhawk would tell me to mind my own business.

Blackhawk had made a friend that managed this particular casino. The guy had become a regular at El Patron, Blackhawk's night club, and was a big fan of Blackhawk's girl Elena with her big salsa band. The guy was always trying to persuade Elena to come perform at his casino, but she was happy where she was. The guy and Blackhawk had been engaged in idle conversation over a cocktail, when he mentioned that the casino slots were being cheated. He couldn't figure out how. Blackhawk said he would look into it and invited me to tag along. So, here we were, playing quarter slots, with me getting my pocket picked.

The girl was a pro. A very young pro, but a pro. She knew where the cameras were, and she knew too many stops behind unsuspecting men would bring security down on her. I stayed back while Blackhawk followed her onto the elevator. I noted every floor the elevator stopped at. When it came back down, I followed an older couple on. They gave me a harsh look when I pressed all the buttons. They got off at the first stop. Blackhawk was waiting when the doors opened at the fourth floor.

"End of the hall," he said. Without waiting, he turned and started down the hall. I followed. I could have grabbed the girl as soon as she took the wallet, but this is how Blackhawk and I have our fun.

He reached the door, and moved to the side, his back against the wall, just out of sight of the peep hole. I knocked. After a moment the light in the peep hole darkened. Someone was looking at me. I put on a nice smile and knocked again.

Whoever was looking at me, hesitated, then I heard voices. I couldn't make out the words, but the tone was inquisitive. The door slowly opened. It wasn't the blondie, but another young girl of about the same age. She had brown hair, and a fading bruise on her cheek bone.

"Yes?" she said.

"Hi there," I said brightly. "I'm told this is lost and found and I'm here to pick up my wallet."

She started to shut the door but I had my foot in it. I shoved it open, which shoved her back. I stepped into the room. Blackhawk stepped in behind me. The blondie was sitting in a chair, where she had been looking through my wallet, but it was the woman on the couch that had both my and Blackhawk's attention.

The woman was tall and slender, wearing tight jeans, and an embroidered blouse. She sat casually, her legs crossed with a tooled boot on each foot. Her hair was blonde, but not as white blonde as blondie. Fashionable streaks highlighted her hair in an expensive looking way. She held a throw pillow on her lap. Her left arm lounged across the top of the couch, the right hand under the pillow.

She began to laugh. "Well, look what the cat dragged in," she said.

"They called her Indigo," Blackhawk said in his best, deep, movie trailer voice.

"Let me guess," I said. "9mm Beretta?"

She laughed again, taking her right hand from under the pillow. In it was a 9mm Beretta. "Good memory."

Blondie was looking from us to her. "You guys know each other?"

"Long, long ago, in a land far, far away," I said.

"You still go by Indigo?" Blackhawk said.

She placed the pistol on the lamp table beside her. "I told these girls my name is Jane."

"Jane isn't your real name?" the brown-haired girl said.

"Neither is Indigo," Indigo said.

This was when I realized that Blackhawk and I knew this woman better than the two girls she was sharing the suite with.

She stood and put the pistol in the small of her back. She moved to a desk that had been set up as a bar.

"What are you boys drinking?" she said. She looked at me, "I don't have Boodles, just Tanqueray," she said.

"Good memory," I said.

"Tanqueray and tonic," Blackhawk said.

"Make it two," I said.

"Make it three," the blondie said.

"Make it four," the other girl said.

"You girls old enough to drink?" I said.

"Fuck you, Jack," the blondie said.

"Not Jack. Jackson," Indigo said as she fixed the drinks. "His name is Jackson. The tall, dark, handsome one is Blackhawk."

The brown-haired girl snorted. "Blackhawk?"

"His real name is Fred," I said. "Fred Littlewanger."

Indigo handed us all a drink. "You two still on the comedy circuit?" She looked at the girls. "There isn't any little wanger to it. Take my word for it."

My eyebrows went up. "Oh, really?"

"We shared a community shower a long time ago," Blackhawk said. He raised his glass to the two girls. "Blackhawk will do. At your service."

"So, what are you now?" I asked Indigo. "Let me guess, you are Fagan and this is your merry band of Artful Dodgers."

"First of all," she indicated blondie with her glass, "this is Simone, and this," she indicated the other girl, "is Nikki. I'm just trying to help them out of a little jam."

"So, you just happen to be here?"

"Believe it or not."

"What kind of jam?" I asked.

Blondie Simone took a drink and looking at it made a face. "We have a bunch of people that are looking for us."

"They're going to kill us for sure," Nikki said. She looked frightened. If it wasn't real, she was a hell of an actress.

"A bunch?" I said, looking at Indigo. "What constitutes a bunch?"

"By definition, more than twelve," Blackhawk said.

"A bunch," Indigo said. She wasn't joking.

2

"So, did you send Miss Simone down to pick my pocket, or is this just some improbable coincidence?"

By now we were seated.

"Coincidence," Indigo said. "Like I said, believe it or not. After the unit broke up, I had no idea where anyone went. I'd heard they'd sent you to Germany to fix your foot." She looked at my foot, grinning. "So, how is the foot?"

"Gone," I said.

She looked at Blackhawk, smiling. "However, somehow I'm not surprised you two are together."

"How did you know I'd lifted your wallet?" Simone said. "I never had anyone catch me before."

Indigo laughed, "Honey, you have never met anyone like these two."

"I'm very sensitive to anyone in my personal space, even in a crowded place," I said. "I was aware of you as soon as you got close."

"He's a very sensitive guy," Blackhawk said.

"How do you know these guys?" Nikki asked Indigo.

"It's a long story," Indigo said. "But this guy," she indicated me, "carried me two miles on his back just to be able to get a shot at a guy that was carrying a bazooka."

I looked at the girls. "She's pulling your leg; it wasn't a bazooka, it was a surface to air weapon. And I made the shot," I said, turning to look at Blackhawk.

"Yes, you did," Indigo said.

"How far would you say the target was from me?"

Indigo finished her drink. "I don't know. Maybe two hundred yards or more."

"See!" I said to Blackhawk. He just smiled.

"Why did you shoot him? The guy with the surface air thingy?" Nikki said.

"As long as that guy was there with his thingy, our helicopter couldn't come get us," Indigo said. "They had us trapped."

"Helicopter?" Simone said.

"It was a long time ago," I said. I looked at Indigo. "What's the story here?" I said, changing the subject.

She shrugged. "I was driving out of Vegas heading east on I-10. I'd been driving a long time, so I pulled off the freeway to make a pit stop. Pick up some fruit and stuff to eat. I was sitting at a stoplight, minding my own business, munching on an apple. Nikki and Simone – I didn't know their names then – were standing at the corner with this big Mexican dude. They were all yelling at each other, when suddenly the dude smacks Nikki and knocks her down."

Nikki's hand went to her bruised cheek.

"No way to treat a lady," Blackhawk said.

"What I was thinking," Indigo said.

"So you decided to get involved," I said, shaking my head. "You were taught better than that."

Indigo shrugged. "I'm out," she said. "There are no rules anymore."

"So, what did you do?" Blackhawk said.

Simone laughed. "We couldn't believe it. She gets out of her car and comes up to Mickey…"

"Mickey your pimp?"

"Our handler," Nikki said.

"Your handler," I repeated. "Then what?"

Simone laughed again. "She asks Mickey if he wants an apple. He looks at her like she's nuts. Mickey calls her a bitch. Then Jane tossed him her apple and, like, just reflexes he starts to catch it and she smacks him up side his head with the butt of her gun."

I looked at Indigo. She was studying her nails.

"Knocked him straight down," Nikki laughed. "I mean, it was funny as hell, but we both knew there would be hell to pay."

"So, Jane says, 'get in' and we got in, and she drove us away. When I looked back the bastard was still sitting on the ground, holding his head."

Nikki looked at Indigo, "She told us her name was Jane. She said she'd drop us wherever we wanted to go, but we had no place to go."

I looked at Indigo. "So, you came here?"

"Hide in plain sight. Best place to hide. Especially, after they told me it wasn't just Mickey. There was a bunch."

"More than twelve?" Blackhawk said.

"Hell, yes," Simone said. "They have people all over the Southwest."

I looked around the room. "Nice place to hide."

Indigo shrugged, "Can't pay for it. I've had a bad run of luck lately," she said. "Used a fake credit card. Figured we'd lay low then sneak out. Simone said she could pick up some walking money." She shrugged. "Okay with me."

"I still can't believe you knew you'd been lifted," Simone said.

"Who has people all over the Southwest?" Blackhawk said.

They were silent.

"They say it's a sex ring," Indigo finally said. "According to the girls, they have a lot of muscle."

"How long you girls been with Mickey?" Blackhawk said.

"Just a couple of weeks," Simone said. "We were both reassigned. Me from Tucson, Nikki from Vegas."

"Reassigned? Sounds like you work for Microsoft or something."

"That's how they ran it. It was a business. I worked at Vegas for six months," Nikki said. "Then they sent me here."

"Who's they? Who runs the business?"

She shrugged and looked at Simone. Simone shrugged. "All I know is that it is a big outfit. Got places in L.A., San Francisco, San Diego, all over. Tucson, Phoenix, even Vegas and Reno. Around here a guy named Luis runs it."

"All West Coast?" I asked.

"Never heard anyone talk about any place east of Phoenix

except Albuquerque. Each place is a pretty sweet gig. Fancy apartments, share it with four or five girls. All kinds of girls. White girls, Hispanic girls, Black girls, small town girls, a lot of them from Europe."

"Eastern European," Nikki said. "I knew a couple of girls from Georgia. Like the country. They had boys too, but they kept them separate. Big cars, designer clothes. Big parties with lots of coke and booze."

"At first," Nikki said.

"Yeah, at first. That's how they sucked you in. Compared to where I come from, and what I come from, it was pretty sweet."

"Julie," Nikki said.

"Yeah, Julie," Simone said. "At first you are with Julie. She's your best friend, takes you to parties and shit. Then she introduces you to men she wants you to be nice to. It wasn't so bad. Most of the men were business types, you know, respectable looking. Actually were clean. She made sure we were checked. You know for STDs and shit."

"What if you didn't want to be nice to the men?"

Simone barked a short, caustic laugh. "That was no option. They'd beat the shit out of you. Or if you became trouble you disappeared. Probably out into the desert in a gully somewhere. You learned real fast that it was better to do what they wanted."

"Like Erin," Nikki said.

"Yeah, like Erin."

"Who's Erin?" Indigo asked.

"Girl that disappeared," Nikki said.

Simone picked her purse up and pulled out a pack of cigarettes.

"I told you, no smoking," Indigo said. "All we need is for a bellhop to walk by and smell it and turn us in to the front desk and there we go, down the rabbit hole."

Simone stuffed her cigarettes back into her purse.

"They had all these places, but only one Julie?" I asked.

She shrugged, "Maybe more, but the only one I ever saw. Julie was the recruiter," Nikki said. "She was high up in the organization. Once she had you broke in, she handed you off to one of the handlers."

"Like Mickey."

"Yeah, like Luis, who gave you to Mickey."

"So, if you had such a great gig, why were you on a street corner?" Blackhawk said.

They were both silent for a moment. Then Nikki said, "Mickey said we were stealing. Not giving him all the money. He tells you to get in the car, you get in the car. He didn't tell us where we were going until we got to that street corner. Then he said as punishment we had to work the street for a week. Blow jobs in the back alley. Teach us a lesson."

I shook my head. "So, were you?"

"Was I what?"

"Stealing."

Simone looked sheepish, "Yeah, not much, but yeah."

"So what do you do now?" Blackhawk asked Indigo.

"Damned if I know," she said.

There was a knock at the door. Nobody moved. I looked at Indigo. She shook her head and picked up the Beretta.

She put it under the pillow. Nikki got up, went to the door and peered through the peep hole.

"Looks like room service," she said.

Blackhawk looked at me and cocked his head toward the bedroom. I followed him in. Indigo was watching us. We both stepped back to where we could see but not be seen. I pointed at Indigo.

"Open the door," Indigo said.

3

The first guy pushing through the door was tall and rangy, wearing an ill-fitting casino jacket. Great disguise except for the jeans, the boots and the cowboy hat. He had a pistol in his hand. He was immediately followed by a big Mexican guy with a bandage on the side of his head and a mouse under his left eye. He also had a pistol. The two men came quickly into the room waving their pistols. They were followed by the third guy. A dapper dandy with a thousand-dollar suit and a seven hundred-dollar Glock.

"Don't nobody move," the cowboy shouted.

Nobody moved.

Indigo sat calmly on the couch, like this happened every day.

The cowboy looked back at the dandy. "She one of yours?"

The dandy shook his head. "Don't know who she is. Probably trying to take your place." He nodded toward Nikki. "You've been a bad girl, Nikki," he said.

"Fuck you, Luis," she said. Frightened but defiant.

"Oh, you've already done that. And now I want my property back."

Nikki just stared at him. "How did you find me?"

Luis smiled. "We can always find you," he said.

"Let's just do'm and get out of here," the cowboy said.

Luis looked at the Mexican. "Shut the door."

The Mexican kicked the door shut.

"Get it over with," Luis said. The cowboy turned and lifted his pistol. Blackhawk and I stepped through the bedroom door.

"Oops," I said.

Everyone froze, the three guys and the two girls turning their heads to look at us. Indigo kept her eyes on the cowboy.

Indigo, Blackhawk and I held a distinctive advantage. We had been trained in the protocols of a close quarter fire fight. As with everything, there was a science to it. If everyone began firing willy nilly, we might all choose to shoot the same guy. That left the not shot to shoot us. So, following our trained protocol, Indigo shot the cowboy through her lap pillow. As he fell, she shot him again. I shot the Mexican. I was in the middle and so was he. Actually, I shot him three times. Must have been the adrenalin. Blackhawk was apparently feeling benevolent. He shot Luis in the knee. Luis screamed and fell to the carpet, his pistol clattering under the coffee table. The shots of all three of us seemed as one.

The explosions were deafening and made my ears ring. I looked at Blackhawk like *what the hell?*

"He didn't look very dangerous," he said.

"Those are the ones that will kill you," Indigo said.

Simone was on the floor, her hands on her ears, rocking back and forth, saying, "Oh my God, Oh my God" over and over. Nikki had her back to the wall, staring at Luis as he writhed on the floor.

Nikki looked to Indigo, then to me. "Who the hell are you guys?"

Blackhawk knelt beside Luis. Luis's eyes were all scrunched closed. He was holding his knee, rocking back and forth, making a high pitched keening sound. Blackhawk took hold of his ear and twisted it sharply. The pain popped Luis's eyes open.

"This is your lucky day," Blackhawk said quietly. "I didn't feel like killing you today. But, make no mistake, if I ever see you again, I will kill you."

He reached inside Luis's jacket and took his phone. I stepped over to the cowboy and the hapless pimp, Mickey, and took their phones. Blackhawk stood. He looked at Indigo. "It's time to go," he said.

"I don't have to tell you, there are surveillance cameras on every floor," she said as she stood.

"I'll take care of it," Blackhawk said. He looked at me. "Take the girls out of here, go through the parking lot and walk until you can't see this place anymore." He pulled his phone and hit a speed dial number. I could hear it connect. I recognized Nacho's voice as he answered.

"Get the band van and wait for Jackson to call," Blackhawk said. He disconnected. "Time to go," he said again.

Indigo must have agreed. She was stuffing everything she

had into a small carry-on piece of luggage.

Blackhawk grabbed Luis by the collar and dragged him through the bedroom door. He slung him into the bathroom. I pulled the dead cowboy into the bedroom, then went back for Mickey the hapless pimp. As I pulled his lifeless body in, Blackhawk was pressing his Sig Sauer against Luis's forehead. Luis looked sick with fear.

"You stick your head out of here, I'll shoot it off," Blackhawk said.

Blackhawk stepped out and closed the door. He moved by me and I closed the bedroom door. Blackhawk went to the front door and opened it carefully. He peered out, checking both ways.

"All clear," he said. He looked at me. "After I take care of the surveillance footage I'll go to the club."

"How are you going to do that?" Nikki said. "Take care of the surveillance stuff?"

"I'll explain later," I said. I took her by the elbow and moved her toward the door. "Time to go."

As I took the girls out into the hallway, Indigo pointed her Beretta at the bedroom door. "That's a mistake leaving him," she said.

"It's my mistake," Blackhawk said steadily.

They looked at each other for a moment, then she shrugged and put the Beretta away. I had the girls on each arm and did my best to saunter down the hall to the elevators. Indigo waited, then followed, pulling the suitcase and looking like the everyday guest. We caught the first elevator, and she waited for the next one.

4

When we stepped off the elevators, we were laughing and having a good old time. We made our way toward the front doors, stopping twice to run my casino card through a slot machine. I didn't win. We moved casually, not anxious, nothing abnormal.

We got lucky. As we reached the front, a group of seniors was disembarking from a shuttle van. I hustled the girls out and timed it so as the last two old ladies stepped off the van, I stepped on. The driver looked surprised. I held a hundred-dollar bill toward him. His eyes widened.

"What's your name?" I asked. Nobody is dangerous that asks for your name.

"Oliver," he said.

"Do you like to be called Oliver, or Ollie?"

"My friends call me Ollie."

"Well, Ollie, I need a very small favor, and I'm willing to pay you a hundred bucks for it."

"What kind of favor?"

"We need a ride. Just a couple of blocks down that outside side street."

"I'm not supposed to…..." he started.

"Only take five minutes," I said, shaking the bill at him. "You'll be right back here in no time."

He looked around, leaned down to look at the casino entrance, then with a quick move, the bill disappeared from my hand. I waved the girls aboard. I could see Indigo coming through the automatic doors.

The driver started to close the van doors. "Hold on," I said. "I have one more."

I stepped down on the last step so Indigo could see me. She walked over, head down and carried her suitcase aboard. As she slid into a seat, she looked at me, cocking her head with a frown.

"Just got lucky," I said.

The driver shut the door and carefully pulled away from the curb. He slowly wound his way through the lot. I directed him out the entrance and had him take the access road that had been built just for the casino. He drove until we had a turn in the road and the casino was no longer in sight. I had him pull to the curb.

We all got off. The van did a U-turn and pulled away. I called Nacho.

"Superboy," he said by way of greeting.

I ignored him. I told him where we were.

"I have no idea where that is," he said. "Lived here my whole life, and never have been out there."

"It's new. Use the GPS on your phone."

"The world's going to technological hell," he said, and I hung up.

The girls were watching me. "Our ride's on the way," I said.

"What club?" Indigo said.

"You'll see," I said.

The girls sat on the curb. I stood and waited. It took Nacho a half hour to get there.

The van turned the corner and came toward us. It was an old blue, faded Chevy that Elena had insisted Blackhawk buy so the band would have something to transport all the instruments and equipment in. Blackhawk had tried to explain to her that she and her big salsa band never played anywhere other than at his nightclub, the El Patron. "You never know," she said.

Nacho pulled the van to the curb beside us. As he swung out of the driver's side, the door screeched as only metal on metal can.

As he came around, I said, "Ladies, this unspeakably ugly specimen is Nacho."

"Superboy is just jealous," Nacho said. He opened the sliding side door for the girls. He picked up Indigo's suitcase. He carried it around to the back and opened the back double-doors.

"As well he should be," Indigo said.

"He's huge," Simone said softly, as if Nacho wasn't right there.

Nacho was large. Next to Nacho, Mickey the pimp would look like a female soccer player. While his waist was small, Nacho's shoulders and arms were massive. His hair was black, glossy and long. His face bore the scars of years fighting the street gang battles. He was Blackhawk's Segundo. His right hand. An ex-con who wanted to go straight but couldn't find anyone to hire him until he met Blackhawk. As he would say, he had done the crime, done the time and didn't want to go back. Neither he nor Blackhawk would ever talk about it, but something had happened that had indebted and bonded Nacho to Blackhawk with a loyalty that only brothers can understand.

We loaded, the girls in the far back, Indigo in the middle and me in the passenger seat. As she climbed in, Nikki said to me, "Does he always call you Superboy?"

"He's just being a smart ass."

As Nacho started the van, Indigo said, "Hey Nacho, why do you call him Superboy?"

I just shook my head.

"Everybody buckled up?" Nacho said. He looked in the mirrors and pulled away from the curb.

He glanced at me and laughed. "Blackhawk don't talk much but every great once in a while he'd talk about this guy. To hear him tell it, Superboy here could do everything but fly."

"Superboy," Indigo laughed, leaning forward and slapping the back of my head.

"Never mind any of that," I said. Looking at Nacho I said, "Take us back to the club. Take the long way. Make sure we're not followed."

He took the van in a wide U-turn and drove back the way we had come. A few moments after we had passed the casino, we were on the access ramp merging onto the southbound 101. We rode in silence for a long time.

Finally, Simone said, "Tell us one of those Superboy stories."

"Yeah, Nacho. Tell us a story," Indigo said.

"I can't," Nacho said. "I'm sworn to secrecy. If I told you, he might have to kill you."

"He'd have to get in line," Simone said.

5

Nacho pulled the van into the El Patron parking lot. The El Patron was a good place in a bad neighborhood. Maybe when Blackhawk had first come to it, it might have fit in, but now it was a little bit of Vegas set in the southside, below the Durango curve. A large two-story rectangular block building with a terra cotta shingle roof surrounded by a large asphalt parking lot. A transformed industrial building that was forty thousand square feet of pulsating fun. The Vegas part was the neon that Blackhawk had recently added. Just to help the uninformed to find it. The surrounding neighborhood was run down. But once you found yourself inside the double doors of the El Patron, if you didn't have fun, it was your fault.

Under one roof were three nightclubs. One was for the country folks who liked their boot scooting and cold tap beer. The other was a nightly psychedelic barrage of Guns and Roses and Aerosmith. Both rooms were heavily insulated to keep the noise inside. At the far end of the hallway that dissected the interior, was the largest of the clubs. This was where Blackhawk's lady, Elena, held forth with her large salsa band. While the other two did okay, this one was packed every night she performed.

Nacho had dropped us at the back-delivery dock where Elena had been waiting. She led us through the storage room, on through the bar and then up the stairs. The stairs led to a landing that had one door. At the end of the landing was a large, window-sized mirror. It was two way. The door opened to the hallway that led to the door of the living quarters and further down, the door to Blackhawk's office, which sported the two-way mirror. Elena opened the door to the apartment and held it as we filed in.

The living area was spacious with expensive furnishings. Elena followed us in and moved to the wet bar that occupied the far corner.

She turned to look at us, especially at Indigo.

"My name is Elena," she said. "This where Blackhawk and I live." She said this with emphasis. "Can I get anyone something to drink?"

No one wanted anything.

"Please sit and make yourselves comfortable, Blackhawk will be here shortly," she said. She looked at me and tilted her head to the other room. She turned, expecting me to follow. I did.

Once in the other room she turned. "What is going on? Who are those people?"

"Didn't Blackhawk tell you?"

"I was drying my hair. He left a voicemail, and now he's not answering his phone. He just said to expect you, he didn't say why. Who are those people?"

"The two young ones are prostitutes. The older one, the one they call Jane, is someone Blackhawk and I knew a longtime ago."

Elena gave me her look. "Maybe you should explain this to me," she said.

So, I did.

I had to hand it to her, she didn't interrupt. When I finished she turned and went into the kitchen. She opened the stainless-steel refrigerator and extracted a bottle of water. She twisted off the cap and tossed it into the stainless-steel wastebasket that was under the sink.

She took a long drink, then looked at me. "So tell me again about the woman you say they call Jane. Like maybe that isn't her name?"

"She was part of our unit," I said.

"The only woman," Elena said. "Blackhawk told me of her. She was called Indigo."

"Yes," I said.

"And now she shows up with these girls?"

"Yes," I said.

"Is she a prostitute?"

"No," I said. "She just met them."

"Just a coincidence?" she said.

This time I didn't say "yes". I shrugged instead.

"Helluva coincidence," she said.

I went back to saying yes.

"And three men busted into their room and were going to shoot them. All three."

"Well, they didn't just bust in. One of the girls let them in."

"Let them in?"

"Accidently," I said.

"You sure?"

Good question. I thought about it. "Yeah, accidentally."

"So now Blackhawk wants to hide them here?"

"I think so," I said. "I haven't talked to him about it."

"With men wanting to kill them, he wants them here?"

I shrugged. "When he gets here, we will find out what he wants."

Elena looked at me a long time. Finally, she said, "Most of the time I am glad you came back into his life." I started to say something. She shook her head. "But sometimes I am not so glad." She brushed by me and went back out to the living room.

6

Elena got them settled into the two guest rooms. The first thing the girls wanted was a shower. Elena made sure they had what they needed, using some of her personal stuff, including a hairdryer. She had a rehearsal, so after she got them settled, she left Indigo and me in the apartment.

"Drink?" I said, moving to the wet bar.

Indigo shook her head, "Maybe later." She watched me as I fixed mine. I fixed a Boodles with a drop of bitters. I stirred it with my finger. She was smiling.

I took a drink. Always delicious. I looked at her. "What?"

She shook her head. "You are thinking this is just too big a coincidence."

"Big coincidence," I agreed.

"Imagine how I feel. What were you two doing at that casino, anyway?"

I took the drink and sat on the oversized couch. "The casino's manager is a fan of Elena's. Sometimes he comes here to watch her perform. He and Blackhawk were talking, and he mentioned he had a problem with someone cheating the slot machines. He asked Blackhawk to look into it. He took me along."

Indigo laughed, "So, Blackhawk didn't just tell him to look for someone with an electro-magnetic pulse jammer?"

I shrugged. "He comped Blackhawk and Elena a suite for the week-end. Free dinner at his restaurant which sports a famous chef. Gave them money to gamble with, all the bells and whistles. No sense in telling him everything at once."

"Copy that," she said. "I guess I will have that drink." She stood and moved to the bar. She studied all it had and finally made her choice. As she mixed a Grey Goose with tonic she said, "What's the story on Blackhawk and Elena?"

I was looking at her. Still slim and fit. Hair was longer and lighter. Minimal make-up. She didn't need it. You'd think a kick-ass Ranger would be kind of butch looking, but not her. Put her in a simple black dress with a string of pearls and she'd be ready for the ball.

"Story is Elena was performing here," I said. "Place was run down, only one saloon. A lot of the building was closed up. Blackhawk stopped in for a drink, and the rest as they say, is history."

"He bought it?"

"As long as she came with it. I think he was buying her as much as the place. I never saw it before, but I'm guessing he put a couple hundred thousand into it."

She walked across the room and sat again. "Where'd he get the money?"

I shrugged. "Never asked."

"You got a couple hundred thou hanging around? I sure don't."

I smiled. "I live a simpler life than Blackhawk."

"Yeah," she said. "You don't have Elena." She looked at me across the rim of her glass. "Or do you? You with someone?"

"Sitting here with you right now."

"No wife, girlfriend?"

I shook my head.

She looked at my foot. "You get along okay?"

"I'm used to it. Why are you out?"

"You got hurt. Blackhawk and the others decided they didn't want a replacement. I got offered a backroom desk job," she laughed. "Can you imagine?"

"So what have you been doing?"

"Kicked around the coast for a while. Ended up in Vegas. You ever heard of Renny Savullo?"

I shook my head.

"Casino guy. Back in the day he was hooked up with what they used to call the syndicate, but now he's straight. I worked for him, doing his security."

"Worked? As in past tense?"

"Yeah."

"But not now?"

"Two things went wrong. I got bored and he thought he was paying for more than security. Ended up a disagreement as to what I was being paid to do."

"What then?"

"Thought I'd take a look at the East Coast. Bought an old junk car with salvage papers. Used another name. Started driving. Decided to take a break, ran into the girls, then ran into you."

"Car's still at the casino?"

"Yeah, I'm done with it. They'll haul it off eventually."

I finished my drink, then set the glass aside. I studied her as she studied me.

Finally, I said, "big coincidence."

"Yep."

"This Savullo guy looking for you, for any reason?"

"Nope."

"He have anything to do with the girls? One of them said she came from Vegas."

She nodded, "Nikki. Naw, he's a casino guy. I know the sex trade is big in Vegas, but he's not into it. Not that I ever saw, anyway."

I was still watching her. "When super slick came through your door with his two gunnys he said Nikki had something of his. What was he talking about?"

She shrugged. She sat her mostly untouched drink aside. "No idea. Ask her."

The door opened, and Blackhawk came in. We watched as he went over to the wet bar and opened a bottle of water.

He turned and looked at us. "You guys want to go down and watch Elena rehearse?"

"Love to," Indigo said. As she stood, the girls came in from the back. Elena had also, somehow, found fresh clothes that fit them. Mostly. They were scrubbed up and without make-up. They looked like what they were. A couple of teenagers. They had dried their hair but not styled it. God, they looked young. They had heard Blackhawk.

"I want to go," Simone said.

"Me too," Nikki said.

Blackhawk said, "Come on then." He moved to the door and opened it, holding it for us.

They started by me toward the door. I stopped Nikki, putting my hand on her shoulder. She looked at me.

"That guy Luis said you had something of his. What is it?"

She looked at me, hesitating. She looked at Simone.

Simone cocked her head. "Tell him," she said.

Nikki looked back to me. "It's my phone."

"He wants your phone? He was going to kill you to get it?"

"Yeah, one time when he was asleep I downloaded his tablet into it."

"So you were with him?" Indigo asked.

She shrugged. "He was the boss. Every once in a while, he'd take one of the girls with him."

"What was on the tablet?" I asked.

Again, she shrugged. "I don't know, but he used it all the time."

"Why'd you download it?"

She looked at Simone. "Figured if I got in a bind, I could use it somehow."

"How'd he find out you had downloaded it?" Blackhawk asked.

She looked sheepish.

Simone ruefully shook her head. She said, "Julie. We were doing some blow with Julie and she was messing with your phone, and that's when you told us. So it was Julie told him."

I looked at Indigo. She was looking at Nikki. I looked at Blackhawk. He was looking at Nikki. I joined the group and looked at Nikki.

"That's how they found us so fast," Indigo said, this time looking at Blackhawk.

7

We were downstairs at the bar. Elena and the band were running through a number, over and over. Elena was a perfectionist.

Jimmy had Nikki's phone. Jimmy was our resident nerd. We were sitting at the rectangular bar. Nacho was across from me at his stool on the corner. Jimmy had his laptop on the bar with a USB cord attached to the phone. He fiddled with the phone for a while. Finally, he said, "All his stuff is password protected."

The girls, Indigo included, were mesmerized by Elena. Blackhawk said above the band noise, "Can you get by it?"

Jimmy shook his head. "Maybe, probably not."

"Can you disable the GPS?" I said.

"I think so," he said. He fiddled some more. After a few minutes Jimmy set the phone on the bar. "Done. GPS is disabled. I've got a friend who could probably get by the password."

"Call him," Blackhawk said. Jimmy pulled out his own phone and dialed. As it connected he moved down the bar.

"You think that organization is going to try to find the girls?"

"Working premise."

"Yeah, somebody whacks your guys and steals your girl, I'd go after them."

"Prepare for the worst," he said.

Jimmy came back. "He's at work today. Says he can come tonight."

I looked at Blackhawk. "We gonna be here that long?"

"When I disabled the GPS," Jimmy said, "I put some addresses into the phone. Right now, the phone's out at Westworld."

"Westworld?" Blackhawk said.

"Big car show out there. Probably several thousand people milling around."

I looked at Blackhawk and he looked at me. "You think that'll do it?"

He said to Jimmy, "You think that'll keep them off our backs?"

Jimmy shrugged, "No guarantee, but it might throw them off."

"I think we should find another place first thing in the morning. Figure out how we're going to handle this."

"We handle it by eliminating the threat," Indigo said, turning to look at us. "You should have done that guy," she said to Blackhawk. He shrugged. "You sure the surveillance tape was taken care of?"

"I erased it," Blackhawk said.

"What guy?" Jimmy said. Then he said, "Never mind. I

don't want to know. My buddy will be in tonight, then we'll know what's on the phone."

Blackhawk looked at Nacho. "Put Duane out front. Tell him to hit the button if he sees anyone that looks out of place."

The button was an alarm that activated a low-light strobe that danced light on the floor behind the bar. It couldn't be seen unless you were behind the bar. It was used to warn Nacho or Blackhawk that something was up at the front door. Blackhawk had installed it after Detective Boyce had taken a bullet in the parking lot.

We all watched Elena practice another hour, then she broke and went up to take her nap. It was her normal routine. Blackhawk followed her. The band came to the bar for a beer. The girls went to explore the nightclub. Indigo sat at the bar with me.

"Think we could get a beer?" she asked, watching the band drink theirs. They all spoke Spanish. My Spanish wasn't that good, but I didn't need to understand their words to see their interest in Indigo. Couldn't blame them.

"Hey, Jimmy," I held up two fingers. In a second, he was setting two Dos Equis in front of us. Indigo waved off the glasses he offered.

Sipping hers, Indigo said, "You think we are safe here?"

I sipped mine. "If they are using Nikki's phone to find us, then probably. If it's something else, then probably not."

She grunted. Then she said, "What happened after you lost your foot? I wasn't on that Op."

"They flew me out to Germany. Stayed there until I

could function. The colonel came to tell me I was out. Told me the unit was dissolved. Asked what I wanted to do, and I said I didn't know, and I didn't."

"So you came back to the States?"

"They gave me some money, not much, but enough to come out here"

"Why here?"

"Arizona?"

She nodded.

"Always had a romantic view of Arizona. You know, cowboys and Indians, the old West. That thing. I wasn't planning on staying but I wanted to see it."

"So you live here?"

"You mean at the El Patron? Hell, no."

She smiled. "Why hell no?"

"Elena wouldn't allow it."

"You don't get along?"

"We get along fine, but she's not keen on sharing Blackhawk."

"I could have told her you two are a package deal."

"Just hooked up again. For the first two years I lived in Phoenix I didn't know he was here too."

She looked at me, surprised, "You didn't know he lived here?"

"Not till the colonel told me."

She laughed, "Don't tell me the colonel is here too?"

I smiled, "No, the colonel is living somewhere in Illinois."

"I heard he was retired."

"From the unit. But, believe me, he's still active. Blackhawk and I just did a small job for him, pulling a guy out of Guatemala."

"He hired you?"

"He has a lot of contacts. Pretty good pay."

"Maybe I could get in on some of that? How can I get in touch with him?"

"I'll call him. See if he wants you to have his number. But understand, if you cause him any trouble you'll have trouble with me. And Blackhawk."

She leaned back and looked at me. "I love that old man. I won't cause him trouble."

"He was pretty hard on you."

"Hell yes, he was. Because I was a woman. The only woman. And he knew what I was up against. He made me do twice as much for twice as long as you guys. But that's why I love him. He made me Indigo. So where do you live?" she said, swallowing the rest of her beer.

"Pleasant Lake Marina," I said.

"On a lake?"

"On a houseboat on a lake."

"A boat?"

"A houseboat."

She grinned. "This I gotta see."

"It isn't much."

She slid off her stool. "No, I mean it. I want to see it. What time does Elena start?"

"Not till nine."

"We have time to kill."

I slid off the stool, dropping a five. "We have time to kill," I repeated.

"Cool," she said.

8

There was a new kid on the shuttle cart. He saw me pull in and park in my slot, so he was waiting as we slid out of the Mustang. The visitors lot was all the way at the top of the hill. The assigned parking for the residents and staff was halfway down. It was still such a long trek that the Marina had shuttles running up and down to transport visitors and their wallets, and residents and their shopping bags. From the parking slot, it was a beautiful view of the large lake. Spreading below were the buildings that made up the large marina bar and gift shop. Roofs white and bright in the sunshine. The gift shop was also a general store which supplied the permanent residents, like me, with staples such as eggs, milk, bread and beer. There were several docks stretching out, including the rental dock on the west side that held multiple boats of various sizes and abilities. Some of the docks were covered. Mine was Dock C. It was uncovered. It housed a number of wet docked pleasure crafts and some houseboats. Most were much newer than my old scow. The previous owner had named my boat *Tiger Lily*. I never changed it. Yeah, I know. When Boyce wanted to irritate me, which was often, she would call me Peter Pan.

Indigo stood beside the shuttle cart the kid was driving. She was looking at the lake.

"It's beautiful," she said. "But I'm used to lakes having green grass and trees all around them."

"Welcome to Arizona," I said. I slid into the cart. Indigo joined me.

The kid dropped us at the bottom. I tipped him. I took her on a short tour of the marina bar, the gift shop mini-mart and showed her the rental dock. I led her through the unsecure security gate and down my dock. Pete Dunn's *Six Episodes* was closed up and shuttered. Pete was a neighbor who bought the boat with the money he had made writing six episodes of a reality TV show. When we reached the Tiger Lily, Eddie's friend Diesel was lying on the dock in front of my boat. Diesel was a large dark mutt of undetermined breed that had showed up at the marina one day. The dog took a shine to Eddie, the marina handyman, and stayed.

I helped Indigo aboard. Diesel thumped his tail, but that was it. He was watching us but didn't raise his head. While Indigo was looking at the dog, I disengaged the LED light that informed me if anyone had been, or was, aboard. It wasn't blinking.

"He yours?" Indigo said.

"Belongs to Eddie," I said. "Eddie lives in that River Runner across the way there." I pointed across the water at another dock. "He's the resident handyman here. But actually, Diesel doesn't belong to anyone."

"The dog just runs free?"

"Maureen likes it that Diesel keeps the geese and ducks off the docks. They make a mean mess. He's the lesser of two evils. If he makes a mess, Eddie cleans it up."

"Maureen?"

"She manages things here."

I opened the sliding door to the lounge and ushered her in. The place smelled musty. I turned the air on. "This is it," I said. "Like I said, not much. I'll give you the tour, if you have twenty seconds to spare."

"Lead on," she laughed.

I stepped into the galley and opened the oversized refrigerator. I pulled two Dos Equis and opened them and handed one to her.

"This is what is called the galley." I moved on into the hallway. I opened the pocket door to the first stateroom. "This is the guest stateroom," I said. "Then the head. Nice big shower. And last but not least, the master stateroom." I moved to the sliding bow doors and slid them open. A breeze immediately hit us.

"I've had apartments smaller than this," she said. "Nice big bed," she said with a smile. "And it's made. You didn't even know I was coming."

"Yes," I said, retreating out onto the bow. "Let me show you the top deck."

She followed me up the outside winding stairs to the top. I slid the aluminum frames of two chaise lounges over to the railing. I collected two cushions from their locker. She was looking out over the lake, then moved over where she could study the marina.

"Which one is the dog owner's boat?"

I moved over beside her. "Not really the owner. They cohabitate." I pointed at Eddie's River Runner.

"Is he home now?" she said.

"If I know Eddie, he's out in his skiff, fishing."

She looked at me. "So you live here all the time?"

"Except when I visit the mansion in Beverly Hills."

She shook her head. "What the hell do you do? I mean for fun."

"I read, I fish, I listen to music."

"Jesus, Jackson, really? I didn't even see a television. And this place isn't exactly close to much."

"Actually, it's only fifteen minutes to Noterra."

"Noterra?"

"It's a large shopping complex at Happy Valley Road. I try to keep it simple."

"And you don't have a woman?"

"You mean a full time, night-time woman?"

She looked at me, cocking her head. "That's a funny way to put it."

"Sorry, just a line from a movie. No, I don't have a woman."

"So you do watch movies?"

"Occasionally."

"Tell me about the job you did for the colonel."

I shrugged. "Not much to tell. He was hired to pull a guy out of a rebel village in Guatemala. So we did."

"Just you and Blackhawk?"

"No, Adam, Echo and Fabian went along."

She looked at me. Pissed. "Well shit, am I the only one not getting in on this stuff?"

I shrugged. "We didn't talk much. We met the day before we went in. We were briefed and outfitted. We went in and did the job. We came out."

"Who was the guy?"

"Nobody."

"Nobody? Someone spent a lot of money to get him out."

"Yeah, a billionaire named Glick. I'm guessing this guy had info Glick didn't want known."

"Yeah, I've heard of Glick. Nothing good. What about the rest of the team?"

I shrugged. "A couple of them stayed in. Most, like me, you and Blackhawk, chose to opt out."

She took a drink of her beer. She looked at the bottle. "I think I'm getting tired of beer. Do you have anything else?"

"What would you like?"

She handed me her bottle. She sat on one of the chaise lounges. "Surprise me," she said smiling.

I went down and poured the beers out and rinsed and placed the bottles in the recycle bin under the sink. I studied the bar, then fixed two whiskey sours. I carried them back up. She watched me as I brought her drink.

She took it and said, "I have to admit, sitting up here in this weather could be addictive."

I turned and looked out across the water. Several

hundred yards away, toward the dam towers, a tiny boat sat bobbing, with a lone figure fishing.

I pointed at it. "That's Eddie, there."

She shaded her eyes and looked to where I was pointing. She took a sip, "You can buy fish at the market."

I sat beside her, on the other chaise lounge. "You belong to Blackhawk's school of thought. He's said the exact same thing."

We were silent for a while. Finally, I said, "Where were you heading? You said East."

"Not sure, just driving. Something would come to me."

"Nobody back East?"

She looked at me, then out across the water, "None of us have family. You know that."

"Doesn't have to be family."

She shook her head, "There's nobody. All my old bridges have burned. How about you? Have you had any steady relationships?"

I shook my head. "Nothing steady," I said, thinking of Boyce slipping in and out of my life. Currently out. "I know it's possible. Look at Blackhawk and Elena."

"The odd couple."

"Works for them."

"But not for you?"

"No, not so far."

She sat her glass on the deck and stood. "Mind if I use the bathroom?"

"The head," I said, automatically. "Don't worry, it's clean."

She smiled. "You were always known as the fastidious one. The old poetry reader."

"No one would steal the centerfold of a poem."

She laughed and went down the stairs.

I watched the clouds skirt across the mountains, a gentle breeze ruffling the water. The next time I looked for Eddie, he had moved. I couldn't find him. After a while I realized that Indigo was still below, and my drink was empty.

I pulled myself up, picked up her glass and went down the steps. As I stepped down on the stern I realized she had pulled the blackout curtains together. She had left the sliding door open. I stepped through the curtains.

She was lying on the king size bed. Naked. Holding a pillow, covering her up. A little. But, no doubt, she was naked.

"I was beginning to wonder how long it would take you to finish your drink."

I stood looking at her. "You sure about this?" I said.

I could see her smile in the dim light. See her smile and a whole lot of other interesting stuff.

"You and I were always aware of each other," she said. "But it was against the rules. I've always wondered," she said. "Haven't you?"

"Oh, yeah."

"Then you came walking into my hotel room."

"More like we burst in," I said.

She lay there looking up at me. Finally she said, "Walk, burst, whatever, so, are you going to make me wait?" She set the pillow aside.

My momma taught me to not keep a lady waiting.

9

Because of extended activity, we arrived back at El Patron later than intended. The parking lot was packed. I wheeled the Mustang around to the back and parked beside the huge *No Parking* signs that were fastened to the big green garbage dumpsters.

"This place is packed," Indigo said.

"It's Elena. She always packs the house."

We walked around the building to the entrance. Duane was standing guard. There were a few smokers lounging against the wall. Blackhawk enforced the no smoking rule inside. The sun had set as we were traveling back south on the Black Canyon, so the lot was illuminated by the new lights Blackhawk had installed. They put off a sharper, brighter light than the old yellow ones. He says that if anyone tries to shoot me in the parking lot again, at least now they'll be able to see me.

Duane held the door for us, nodding at me. We made our way down the hallway to the last door. Blackhawk had spent a lot of money sound proofing all three nightclubs.

You could barely hear the music in the hall. However, when we went through the double doors into Elena's place the din was off the charts.

Elena had the crowd moving. She was in the middle of *La Charreada*. The dance floor was a moving, pulsing thing. In the middle were Simone and Nikki. Each had snagged a young Hispanic man and was giving him a run for his money.

I moved through the crowd. Indigo followed closely. Blackhawk was behind the bar with Jimmy and Nacho. They were very busy. Blackhawk waved a hand, beckoning us down to the end of the bar. He leaned over and spoke to two young men. They reluctantly relinquished their stools. They smiled brightly at Indigo. No smile for me. My feelings were hurt.

Blackhawk took our drink orders. Indigo ordered another whiskey sour. I got a club soda with lime. He was soon back and set them in front of us. I sipped mine. I was watching Nikki and Simone on the dance floor.

Indigo looked at me and smiled. "Tequila?" meaning that while we were gone, the girls had found the tequila bottle.

I nodded, watching Nikki twirl the kid she was with. "It's a known fact," I said, "tequila makes you a much better dancer."

"Speaking from experience?"

"Unfortunately."

Indigo was watching Elena and her big band. "She is really very good," she said. "She'd make a fortune in Vegas."

I shrugged. "Everyone knows it, including her, but she's happy here. She doesn't have those kinds of ambitions. Here, she runs things, no one to please but herself."

"What about Blackhawk?"

I smiled, "Blackhawk's smart enough to stay out of her way. And he's okay with whatever she does."

"Even if she quit entertaining?"

"Wouldn't blink an eye."

A table opened up behind us, against the wall. I slid off my stool and took it. Indigo joined me. At the next break, the girls joined us. They were flushed and glassy-eyed.

I slouched back in my chair, my legs stretched out. Simone leaned down, putting her face about six inches from mine. "Hey Jackshon honey, you wanna dance?"

I laughed. "You know it's rude to ask a one-legged man to dance," I said.

She looked at me very solemnly. She nodded slowly. "Yeah, that big guy said you only had one foot." She scooted a chair, so she could watch the dance floor while she sat. "Is that true?"

I leaned over and pulled up my pant leg. She leaned forward and looked at the prosthetic.

"Damn," she said. She folded her arms on the table and laid her head on her forearms.

I looked at Indigo and she smiled and shrugged.

Toward midnight a young man sporting really thick glasses came in and stood looking around. He and his briefcase didn't look like they belonged in this place. He spotted Jimmy and made his way through the dancers to the end of the bar. I watched as Jimmy showed him Nikki's phone. The kid opened his briefcase and pulled out a laptop. They moved to the back and put their heads together.

Elena was always prompt at closing time. She felt it was unfair to the musicians to keep them overtime. She paid them a fixed wage, so at precisely one o'clock the music stopped. The bar quit serving ten minutes before that. Tonight, Jimmy and his friend were still working on the phone. Simone was at the table with us, her head down on her arms. Nikki was leaning back against the wall. Her eyes were closed.

I was tired, but I got up to help Nacho and Blackhawk clean up. I straightened tables and chairs and collected glasses and set them on the bar. Indigo joined me, and I caught Elena looking at her, then at me. She arched her eyebrows. I ignored her and continued collecting glasses.

We stacked the glasses on the bar where the morning cleaners would take care of them. Most of the musicians carried their instruments home. When they were playing the next night, the drummer, the keyboard player and a couple others left their equipment here. But on the last night of the three-day run, like tonight, they tore down and took their instruments. Elena always felt obligated to help them. So she was carrying a snare drum out for the drummer.

I drifted over to Jimmy and his friend.

"Any luck?"

Jimmy looked up. He shrugged. "Getting closer," he said. His buddy looked at me. "This is Jackson," Jimmy said. "Jackson, this is Bill. Bill Brown." I put my hand out and he took it.

"So, you are the computer genius?" I said.

"No genius," he said. "But I work for a cyber security company, so I know more than most."

"Appreciate you helping," I said. "Don't let me interrupt."

The kid started working on the computer again.

"He's got a keylogger program that captures keystrokes," Jimmy said.

"Ardamax. The problem is sorting through all the crap that's on this computer. Is this yours?" Bill said, looking at me.

"Not mine."

"Well, whoever it is, this guy's been moving money between at least ten different banks. What does this guy do?"

"Sex trade," Jimmy said.

The kid looked up, his eyes wide behind the coke bottle lenses. "No shit?"

"No shit," I said. "So, this keylogger thing, it lets you know what key strokes have been made on the computer? Or, in this case, phone?"

"Same thing, since the computer was downloaded onto it. The trick is getting it narrowed down to the key strokes used for the password."

"It's getting late," I said. "You think you can get it done tonight?"

"I'm close," he said. He looked at Jimmy. "You said you disabled the GPS?"

Jimmy nodded. "Yeah."

"Well, almost. This phone has a *find phone* app. And it's signed in to the Icloud. What that means is that someone that has the app can still find it."

Jimmy looked at me.

"Shit!" I said. I turned and walked toward Blackhawk, who was mopping where someone had spilled a glass. Before I got to him, the double doors swung open with a bang. Five men in dark clothes came in. They all carried AR-15's.

The man in the middle had a brace on his leg. He had Elena by the hair and a gun to her head. It was Luis.

10

Two of the men pointed their guns at the ceiling and opened fire. Even in the good-sized room, the explosions were deafening. Pieces of the ceiling rained down. I took two long steps and grabbed both girls, slinging them to the floor. They went down screaming. I fell, rolling against the bar, knocking stools out of the way. Indigo was down flat. Blackhawk was on the other side of the bar. I couldn't see him. No worries, he was armed with a mop. Nacho had rolled across the bar to the interior. For an old gang banger he had good instincts.

There was a sawed-off shotgun behind the bar. It had never been pulled because Nacho was usually enough. Not this time. This was bad. Jimmy and his friend were frozen at the end of the bar.

Lying flat, I watched as Luis forced Elena into the room. He was hobbling. "Nikki," he shouted. "Where are you, bitch?" He fired his pistol into the ceiling, then pointed the pistol at Elena. "Bring me the phone!"

I glanced over at Nikki and she had rolled against the

wall, her face in her hands.

"I have the phone," I heard the voice on the other side of the bar. Jimmy.

I came up to my knees as Jimmy came out of the bar, holding the phone up. He moved toward the men. I slipped the Smith and Wesson out of my ankle holster. It was for close work. As far as they were from me, I would have as much luck throwing beer glasses at them.

"Give it to Nikki," Luis demanded.

Jimmy hesitated, then moved over to the girls. I could tell he had forgotten which one was Nikki. Now, Nikki was sobbing uncontrollably. She slowly came to her feet. Jimmy offered her the phone and she took it. With her head down, she slowly moved toward Luis. She sobbed so hard, she was hiccupping.

Luis released Elena's hair. Without looking at her, he poked the side of her head with the pistol. "You move, you die," he said.

Elena's hand went to the side of her head. Her eyes were on Blackhawk. He stood against the wall, still holding the mop. His eyes were on Luis. They didn't waver. Like me, he was too far away to do anything.

Nikki handed Luis the phone. He put it in his back pocket. He turned to the man on his right.

"Take them out of here," he said.

That man and another took Elena and Nikki by the arms and walked them out the door. Elena was looking over her shoulder at Blackhawk. Luis pointed his gun at Blackhawk.

"You should have killed me," he said.

"I will, yet," Blackhawk said.

I pointed the pistol at Luis. Not having much faith, I pulled the trigger. Nacho rose up from behind the bar firing the shotgun. He was five feet away and my left ear went deaf. I began firing as rapidly as I could. The two men flanking Luis flinched and ducked back to the door. Luis went low and scuttled after them. The three of them getting through the door looked like Keystone Cops.

Blackhawk and I rushed the door. Indigo came off the floor like the lithe animal she was and was right behind. She had a pistol in her hand.

"Don't shoot," Blackhawk yelled. "You might hit Elena!"

We reached the door and flattened against the wall on either side. I reached across and pulled the door open. Immediately, bullets were flying, tearing the door to shreds. Indigo reached across me and fired two rounds down the hall.

"Goddammit, I said, don't fire," Blackhawk said.

"She was aiming at the ceiling," I said. "Just keeping them honest."

"One man could keep us here for a long time," Indigo said.

"The Mustang's out back," I said, and before I finished saying it, we were moving.

As he went by, Blackhawk called to Nacho, "Get the girl upstairs! No cops."

Blackhawk burst through the delivery door sending the alarm into a frenzy. I had the key fob in my hand and was unlocking the Mustang as we reached it. Indigo piled into the back, with Blackhawk sliding into the passenger seat. I fired the machine and ripped backward, peeling rubber. I shoved it into gear and the GT S550 kicked us through the parking lot, sliding sideways around the corner.

Just in time to see a large dark SUV ripping out of the lot. I slowed down. Letting it move down the street.

"What are you doing?" Indigo said.

"We're going to follow them," Blackhawk said. "If we press them, they might hurt the girls."

I angled across the lot, so I came at them indirectly. I wouldn't be in their rearview mirror. I bounced over the curb. I let the SUV get two blocks ahead. Good news, bad news. It was late, and traffic was light. Easy for me to keep them in sight, easy for them to spot me. I dropped further back, intermittently turning the lights on and off. The SUV traveled east, bouncing up to Southern. It turned north on Seventh and headed downtown. I followed, well back. We went over the bridge by the baseball stadium. A mile down the road, he darted into the on ramp at I-10. I had to get closer. He zig-zagged between the behemoths that fill the highways every night. I came down the ramp and angled into the nighttime traffic. I had to dodge the big eighteen wheelers. I was slowed by three trucks that relieved their boredom by traveling abreast, blocking traffic. By the time I broke free I watched the SUV swinging up the ramp to AZ51. I couldn't get over fast enough and we sailed by.

"There he goes," Blackhawk said matter of factly. His voice was calm. I glanced at him. I know he was anything but calm inside.

"Take Washington," Blackhawk said.

It was a maddening few minutes until I could take the exit and get going back the other way. I grabbed the AZ51 on ramp. We came down in a glut of traffic merging from the 202. Of course, the SUV was nowhere in sight. We drove on, hoping beyond hope.

Nothing.

"We need to call Jimmy and see if his friend got anything off of the phone," I said.

"Find a place to pull over," Blackhawk said.

"Find a place a girl can use the restroom," Indigo said.

I took the Bethany Home Road exit. At the next light there was an all-night El Pollo Loco. I pulled into the parking lot. Blackhawk got out to let Indigo out. I pulled my phone and started to call Nacho when Blackhawk's phone started vibrating. He answered it as he slid back into the Mustang.

"Yes," he said into the phone. He listened a moment. "No, we lost them." He listened more. He turned and looked at me. "The phone Jimmy gave Nikki to give Luis was his phone."

"Whose?"

"Jimmy's." He almost smiled. "He said that Nikki's was the exact model of his, so he gave Nikki his own phone, so we could keep hers. Said it seemed like a good idea at the time."

I smiled. Atta boy Jimmy. I leaned back thinking.

Indigo came back, and Blackhawk stepped out while she slid into the back.

"So what now?" she said.

Blackhawk looked at me.

"Well, they have to be going somewhere," I said. "Let's just find out where."

"How do we do that?" Indigo said.

I reached for Blackhawk's phone and he handed it to me.

"Jimmy, it's Jackson," I said into the phone. "Can you track your phone?"

There was silence. "Yeah, probably, it's got the same stuff on it that Nikki's had. Give us a second."

I could hear him talking to Bill Brown.

It seemed like forever, but he finally came back on the line. He was excited.

"Got'm! They are stopped on Cave Creek Road. Says it's 11434 north."

"Stay close to the phone," I said and disconnected. I fired the Mustang, went out of the lot, through a red light and roared north on 16th Street.

11

The address was north of Dunlap on Cave Creek Road. The traffic was light. I blew through any lights that came at me. A block away from the address I pulled to the curb, then slowly moved up until we were across from it. The address was a two-story building. It was long and rectangular. The upper half had an outside balcony with a railing. There were no indications as to what the second story was used for. The bottom half was a gun shop. The steps to the second floor were on the outside, at the other end of the building. The building didn't face the street but was at a ninety-degree angle. The building faced east with an asphalt parking lot stretching out in front of it. On the other side of the parking lot, at the back of the lot, there was another two-story building, same as the first. Except it faced the street. In front of it was a small free-standing building that advertised it sold vintage clothing.

The parking lot was empty. No SUV. The place looked deserted. I called Jimmy.

He answered on the first ring. "You still see your phone on Cave Creek Road?"

"Yeah, it's just sitting there."

"There isn't anyone here," I said.

"That phone is," he said. I disconnected.

Indigo leaned forward, her elbows on the backs of our seats.

"Doesn't look like a sex den," she said. "Of course, neither of you bozos know what a sex den would look like."

I looked at Blackhawk. He was studying the property across from us. He looked grim.

"Cambodia," I said.

He didn't seem to have heard me. Then he said, "Yeah, Cambodia. That was a sex den."

"How come I missed all the good ops," Indigo said.

Behind the gun shop was a street that paralleled it and disappeared up a steep incline.

"Let's take a look," I said. I turned the wheel and with a small U-turn, I pulled across Cave Creek and up the incline. I went past the building and pulled over. I popped the trunk and we climbed out. The light of the trunk lid revealed a metal box with keypad styled buttons on it. I pushed the buttons in a particular order and the lid to the box popped open.

"Why don't you just put a neon sign out," Indigo said, looking at the trunk light.

"I'm retired," I said. "I'm just an ordinary citizen now," I said as I pulled out the Kahr .45 and the Mossberg 500 Tactical shotgun. I handed the shotgun to Blackhawk, and then a box of shells. He filled his jacket pocket. Indigo pulled her Beretta as I racked a shell into the Kahr.

The back of the building was dark, in fact the whole block was dark and empty. I pointed to our left. "You two take that side, I'll go around the street side."

"That's where the light is," Indigo said.

"You can do it if you want."

She smiled. "No, I'm good." She patted Blackhawk on the shoulder, "Come on Chief, let's go find your girl."

Blackhawk turned without a word and started into the darkness. I turned, and moving close to the building, I worked my way to the corner. The only light was coming from the street-light across the street. I went around the corner, feeling exposed, and moved cautiously toward the parking lot. If I got caught here the only cover was two decorative boulders that were too small for me to hide behind.

When I reached the corner, I hesitated. Nothing moved. The very occasional car drove past. The thought that they might call the cops crossed my mind. Probably not. Not in this neighborhood. I stood listening. Sometimes you just know a building is empty. But you don't want to stake your life on it. I went slowly around the corner and crouched under a barred window. I cautiously looked inside. It was dark, the window was dirty, and I couldn't see anything. Sometimes you see movement rather than an actual something. I saw nothing. Across the lot, I saw Blackhawk move to the building. He crouched by the stairway that led upstairs. He started up. Now I saw Indigo by the dumpster. She was just a dark form. I could tell by her silhouette that she was covering Blackhawk.

I stepped away from the building and pointed the Kahr up at the upstairs landing. Blackhawk moved to the door. I waited for him to wave Indigo up, but he didn't. He kicked the door in and went inside. Indigo burst away from the dumpster and ran up the stairs two at a time.

I ran out into the parking lot, trying to cover the whole building with one pistol. Indigo went through the door, Beretta ready. I stood waiting. Nothing moved; all I heard was my own breathing.

After what seemed like forever, Indigo came back out on the landing. She gave me a thumbs down. She started down and Blackhawk came out and followed her. They came over to me. In the faint glow of the streetlight from across the street Blackhawk's face was impassive but I knew he was disappointed.

I walked toward them, and my prosthetic foot kicked something. I looked down.

It was a phone. Dark in the night, against the dark asphalt. I picked it up and thumbed it on. A selfie of Jimmy stared at me.

"It's a trap!" I said.

12

They came out from behind the vintage clothing building, firing. Blackhawk, Indigo and I scattered in three different directions. Like quail. This was training. Bunch together and a bunch gets shot. Scatter individually and it will lower the number of casualties. But these guys weren't as coordinated as we were. They were both shooting at me.

The stairs were closer than where I had come from. I skidded around the corner and went to ground hard, behind the stair. Their bullets were chewing up the stucco. I thought of Butch Cassidy and the Sundance Kid. "What's wrong with those guys?" I looked at *those* guys: they were behind the dumpster.

I crawled back to the corner and from ground level, I peered back around the corner, the Kahr in my left hand so I could fire without exposing myself. We had been taught both hands. Spent a lot of time on the range shooting lefty. These guys were blowing up everything in sight. Raking building and across the lot, punching holes into the dumpster. Automatic rifles empower a man. Makes him feel invincible. But like every weapon, they only hold so many rounds. The idiots both went empty at the same time.

They kicked their magazines out and were trying to jam in new ones when Indigo stepped out and started firing. I couldn't see Blackhawk, but I heard the boom of the Mossberg from the other side of the dumpster. He was probably too far away to do damage, but the sound was scary.

Indigo emptied her clip at them, and the guy closest to me went down. The other guy turned and bolted across the street. There were two small dark buildings across from us. The compound was surrounded by a fence with circles of razor wire at the top. Work trucks were parked inside. East of this was a two-story building. It only had a chain across the driveway, but no fence. This is what the guy was running towards. I opened fire, but it would have required enormous luck to hit a moving target at this distance. I didn't have the luck. He ran the length of the building and disappeared into the dark of the far side.

I stood and cautiously moved toward the fallen man. He was alive. He was moaning. I reached him at the same time a black SUV came roaring out from behind the building across the street. It ripped north. No way to get to the Mustang and catch it. Indigo and Blackhawk came up beside me. Indigo and I were reloading. You always reload.

Blackhawk squatted down beside the guy. The guy was gasping, blood bubbling out of his mouth.

"Sucking chest wound," Indigo said. She didn't sound very sympathetic.

Blackhawk looked at me. "Guy's still conscious." He

turned back to the guy. "Where is Luis and the girls?"

I could tell by the look in the guy's eyes he was defiant. His eyes flitted from Blackhawk to Indigo and back.

I squatted down on the other side of the guy. I reached out and pinched his nose. He was struggling to breathe, blood bubbling out of his mouth.

"You picked a bad area to get shot. This is all industrial. There isn't anyone here. No one to call the cops. There are gangs up and down this area. If someone did hear something, they're not going to stick their nose into it." I released his nose. "So, the choice I have is we walk away and someone finds your body in the morning, or you tell me what I want to know, and I'll call an ambulance."

Right on cue, Indigo said, "He ain't worth it. Let's leave him and chase that SUV."

The guy's eyes went to Indigo. Men aren't used to a woman being cold hearted. I could have told him about the Blackfeet Indians who turned their prisoners over to the women. Blackhawk was impatient, he stepped on the man's chest and pushed down on the wound.

"Where are Luis and the women?"

The guy made a strangling noise in his throat and his eyes rolled back in his head. Blackhawk stepped back. The guy had his eyes scrunched shut. When he opened them again, I moved over him, making sure he was looking at me. "You see, what my friend is trying to point out is that we don't have to leave you to die. We can do it right here."

"Where are Luis and the women?" Blackhawk said. "Last chance."

The guy was really struggling for breath. I didn't think he was going to last long enough.

Finally, he struggled something out I didn't understand. I looked at Indigo.

"I think he said something about Union Hills."

It was a street north up the road. I tapped his chest and made him groan. "What else? Where on Union Hills?"

"Cave Creek," he bubbled.

"Come on," Blackhawk said, turning.

Indigo and I followed. We got to the Mustang and I handed Jimmy's phone to Indigo as she climbed into the back seat.

I slid into the driver's seat. "Call 911. You heard gun shots in the 11,000 block of north Cave Creek."

"You're just a softy," she said, and made the call. I didn't wait for Blackhawk to buckle up. As soon as the door shut I just ripped around the corner and out onto Cave Creek Road. As I raced by, I glanced at the guy lying flat in the parking lot. He wasn't moving.

As I drove I tried to remember what was on the corner of Cave Creek and Union Hills. Then I remembered. Oh yeah, that. That makes sense.

13

"The Candy Factory," I said.

"You have a sweet tooth?" Indigo said, leaning up between us.

"It's a strip club," I said. "It's at the corner of Union Hills and Cave Creek."

"I didn't take you for a titties and beer kinda guy," Indigo said.

I ignored her. Blackhawk was staring straight ahead. He had the shotgun between his knees. He awkwardly turned it around and fed shells into it. When it was loaded he pulled his Sig Sauer from his hip holster and dropped the magazine out of it. He racked the shell out of the chamber. Deftly caught it in mid-air and fed the shell back into the magazine. He snapped the magazine into place. He racked the shell into the chamber. He was going to war.

Cave Creek Road was quietly coming awake. The light was gradually seeping from the eastern horizon. There is something about a sunrise that makes the world feel it is fresh and new and is birthing new life. As I drove, the streets became slowly busier. The gas stations were filling with work trucks and worker drones in bright yellow and orange work shirts. They began their day at first light. These were the workers that made their living doing the things most people wouldn't do. Mowing and trimming, manual labor construction work, and city road maintenance. The gas stations of my youth had long since evolved into mini restaurants, that made more money on coffee, fountain drinks, cigarettes, and ready-made sandwiches than on gasoline. Instead of filling their water jugs at home, the workers found it easier to buy their water at the gas station oasis. I wonder what my grandfather would have thought of buying water.

I pushed our speed, with one eye out for the night shift patrolman that still lurked along the main thoroughfares. Just on the north side of Bell Road, Cave Creek Road quickly turns from three lanes to two. I got caught behind a landscape rig, a beat-up truck pulling a high sided trailer. In no hurry to get to their first job. A pick-up with flats of tile in it blocked me from the other lane.

Blackhawk zipped his window down and it startled me. For a brief moment I thought he was going to lean out and start shooting. I guess he just wanted the fresh air.

I finally got around the rig and ran the light at Grovers. The Candy Factory was on the northeast corner up ahead. We were coming up on the southeast corner, where there was an all-night Walgreens. I bounced into the Walgreens lot and pulled into a space that faced the strip club across the street. There two vehicles in the lot. They were illuminated by photo cell activated pole lamps and the burgeoning sunlight. Neither was the SUV.

"Couple of the ole' boys got too drunk to drive home," Indigo said.

I nodded. "That's not our guys."

"What now?" Indigo said.

I studied the building. My gut said it was empty. The front door sported a canopy, like the up-scale hotels near Broadway in New York. I guess they thought it made the place look elegant. All they needed was a doorman. The east side had a handicap ramp up to a single door. Behind the ramp was a fenced area, probably for the garbage bins. The west side was facing Cave Creek Road.

"Strike hard, strike fast," Blackhawk said.

"My gut says there's no one home. The SUV isn't here."

I looked at Blackhawk, and he looked at me. "We look," he said.

"Indigo," I said, "you cover the front door. Blackhawk, you go right, I'll go left."

"That's where the street light is," Indigo said.

"You can do it if you want," I said.

"No thanks hero, I'll pass," she said with a smile.

I backed the Mustang up and turned around. I went back out the entrance, hit the accelerator and ripped across the intersection. I didn't even notice if the light was green. With squealing tires, I pulled into the strip club entrance and jammed the brakes to end up directly in front of the canopy. Any closer and I would have knocked it down. I jammed the Mustang into park and bailed out my door, Blackhawk bailed out his. As I went around the building I glanced back. Indigo was behind the Mustang, arms extended, her Beretta resting on the roof, pointing at the door.

My side of the building was bright from the street-lights. The wall was blank. No doors, no windows. I rushed to the corner and peered around it. There were no lights here, just the ambient light of the street. Down at Blackhawk's end there was the fenced area for the garbage dumpster. I waited a second for Blackhawk to show, but he didn't. I went to his corner and looked around. Blackhawk had the big lid of the dumpster up and was looking inside. I joined him.

Inside was a body. It was a girl. It was Nikki and she was dead.

While he held the lid, I reached inside and felt the pulse in her neck, just to make sure. Nothing.

Indigo had joined us. "Poor kid," she said quietly.

"There's an outside door," Blackhawk said, gently letting the lid down. He turned and went up the ramp to the door. We followed. Nothing to be done about Nikki. This door had a knob with a lock. The easiest kind to break into. It took Blackhawk less than thirty seconds.

We went in ready, but we all knew the place would be empty. It smelled of cheap perfume and spilled beer. There was an undercurrent of marijuana. It was sad, dark, and empty. Men came here came looking for something, wanting something. They always left without it.

Despite the gloom we moved swiftly. If, by chance, there was someone inside they already knew we were coming. Blackhawk moved left, I moved right. Indigo hung back.

When nothing happened she came in, moving to the middle of the room. Right inside the door Indigo said, "Hey, what's this?" She leaned down and picked something off the floor. I couldn't see what she was holding. Blackhawk moved over and took it from her hand.

"It's Elena's bracelet," he said.

"She dropped it on purpose," I said.

Blackhawk put it in his pocket. We went back outside.

"They still have Elena," Blackhawk said. "Or they'd have done them both here."

We walked around to the Mustang.

"What now?" Blackhawk said as we climbed in.

I thought about it.

"This Luis guy probably has places like this all over town. When the guy in the SUV warned them, they took off to another one. Leaving Nikki in the dumpster."

"Why not both of them?" Indigo said. "Why not Elena too? You think she's still alive?"

I looked at Blackhawk. He had a look I'd never seen before. It wasn't pretty. "Because I want to believe it," I said. "And because I'll bet she has told Luis that if something happens to her, Blackhawk and I will spend the rest of our lives hunting him down." I glanced at Indigo in the rearview mirror. "And if Luis is smart, I'll bet he has figured out that Elena is valuable and worth something to trade."

"So where do we look?" Blackhawk said.

I started the engine. "The 101 is three-quarters of a mile up the road. Let's jet back to the bar and see what Jimmy and his buddy have come up with from Luis's tablet."

"What about Nikki?" Indigo said.

"She's gone," Blackhawk said. "Nothing we can do for her."

"They put her in the dumpster on purpose," I said. "I'd bet money that garbage pick-up is today. Once a body gets to a landfill, it's never found."

"Goddammit!" Blackhawk said. "He's a dead man."

I started toward the street, "Yeah, I know that, and you know that, but he doesn't know that. He still thinks he's in charge."

"Tick tock," Blackhawk said.

I pulled out of the lot and ran toward the 101.

14

We were upstairs. Bill Brown had left, Jimmy was on the couch in Blackhawk's office and Simone had cried herself to sleep in the spare apartment bedroom. Nacho had sprawled on the living room floor, hugging a couch pillow and was sound asleep.

Jimmy woke up when we came into the office. Nikki's phone and a laptop were on Blackhawk's desk. Like the kid he was, Jimmy stood, yawned and stretched. Blackhawk went around the desk and dropped into his chair. Indigo took Jimmy's place on the couch, stretched out and closed her eyes. I sat in the high back chair.

I was tired. Indigo was tired. Everyone was tired. Blackhawk looked fresh as a daisy. He beckoned to Jimmy.

"What did you guys find?" he said.

"Guy pays his taxes," Jimmy said. "At least the taxes his accountant says he owes. He runs something he calls Premium Import Export. Based here in Phoenix. Address is a P.O. Box. It's owned by something called Sussex Financial in LA. Money comes into Premium, goes out to several banks, never in amounts of more than nine thousand nine hundred and ninety-nine dollars. Bill says this avoids reporting laws. Then it finally ends up at Sussex where it disappears into the hundred million in investments they manage including their off-shore accounts."

"You guys found all that out?" I said.

"Bill does this stuff. He's very, very smart."

"How does that help me find Elena?" Blackhawk said.

"Probably doesn't. I'm just giving you some background."

Blackhawk waved a hand. "Sorry, go on."

"What might help," Jimmy continued, "is that this guy's tablet has a list of businesses that do business with Premium Import Export. There are eight of them that do the majority of the business."

There was a tablet of yellow-lined paper on the desk. Jimmy picked it up and handed it to Blackhawk.

"Here are the eight."

Blackhawk looked at the list.

"What you are looking at are the business names and corresponding principles that are listed in the Corporation Commission of Arizona. They are all "S" corps. Luis Portofino is listed as at least a part owner in all of them."

"Eight places," Blackhawk said, looking at me. He handed me the tablet. I took it and leaned back. By the names, it appeared they were all strip clubs or bars. Names like "Cheeta Club," or "Playmates." Of course they were. People in the sex trade business don't ordinarily hang out at Tractor Supply.

"The question is," I said, "which is the magic one? We

get one chance, so we better hit the right one first." I looked at Jimmy. "Go next door and wake Nacho up, get him over here."

He went out. Blackhawk was watching me. "She's at one of these," I reassured him. "Where else would they go? Little Luis thought his guys would whack us at the gun shop. When they didn't, and we let that guy get away, they split the Candy Factory. They ran to someplace. Someplace he doesn't think we know about." I looked at the tablet. "It has to be one of these. I'd bet on it."

"You're betting Elena's life," he said evenly. He looked away and shook his head. He took out Elena's bracelet and looked at it for a long moment. Over the last two years I had been becoming aware of the changes in both of us. The colonel had drilled us and drilled us with our commitment, until it was a part of our DNA. The team was the only thing, but the team was expendable to the task. Only your team-mate mattered, unless it came down to your team-mate or the task. Then it was the task. No one outside mattered. We were never allowed *relationships*. We never thought of them.

But now we were out, living lives we never thought imaginable. I could never have dreamed of Blackhawk with someone like Elena. Not long term. But now, here we are. And I watched him look at the bracelet and I knew we would never rest until she was back and safe. And Luis was no longer.

Nacho and Jimmy came in. Indigo was stretched out, leaving no space for them to sit. She was buzzing in a very gentle manner. Nacho looked at her and smiled. Jimmy moved to the wall and leaned on it. I handed the tablet of paper to Nacho. He looked at me quizzically.

"You recognize these places?" I said.

He looked at it. He looked at me. "Yeah, strip joints. Back in the day, I worked at most of them."

"You were a stripper?" I smiled.

"Damn good one," he said.

"Ask him the questions," Blackhawk said, curtly.

"What do you need to know?" Nacho said.

I nodded and opened my mouth. Before anything came out, Indigo slowly sat up.

"You were a stripper?" she said to Nacho, yawning.

"He was a bouncer," I said. "He just thinks he's funny."

"Get to it," Blackhawk said.

"Sorry," I said. I turned to Nacho. "The dick-wad that took Elena owns all of these clubs. I think he has Elena at one of them the question is which?"

Nacho studied the list. He sat beside Indigo. At last he handed me the list back. "Two of them, the last two, I never worked at. The rest of them all have office space and changing rooms besides the main area. The one on Grand Avenue, it's underneath an overpass, used to be like this place. Had more than one venue. They had country upstairs and hard rock downstairs. Then they closed it and a few months later it opened as a strip club. Called it the North Woods Bush Club. That's when I worked there. The strip part was upstairs. I never went downstairs, but that's where the girls changed, and I know there was some kind of mini apartment down there because the managers stayed down there and sometimes would take a girl down there."

"Managers? More than one?"

"One at a time. None of the managers lasted very long. Usually they were cheating the girls out of their tips. Girls were harder to come by than managers. A good stripper, who knew how to work the men, could make several hundred a night."

"Maybe I should check into that?" Indigo said.

Nacho looked at her. "Yeah, you could do it. You're a little old, but not too old yet."

She looked at me. "Can I just shoot him?"

"Maybe later, we need him now."

"So, this Bush Club is where you think they would take Elena?" Blackhawk said.

"Like I said, I don't know about the last two on your list, but if you were going to keep someone for a while, that would be the likely place. At least for what's on that list," Nacho said.

Blackhawk looked at me. "How do we know for sure?"

I shook my head. I didn't like it.

"We can't just go blundering in without getting Elena hurt. First, we need to be absolute that she's there. Second, we need to know the layout. And not least, we need to know what opposition to expect."

"I can tell you how it's laid out," Nacho said. "At least, the way it was when I worked there."

"You haven't been there since the downstairs was remodeled," I said.

He shrugged.

"We need someone to go in," I said.

"That would be me," Indigo said.

"Luis has seen you," Blackhawk said.

I said, "She's right. Luis saw the two girls he was looking for, then he saw you and me. She was just another woman sitting on the couch."

"Until she shot that guy."

"There is that."

Indigo grinned, "I can do it. New hair, new makeup. Just like the good old days, right boys?"

"We do have another option," I said.

They looked at me. "They have Elena, and if they were going to kill her they would have done it when they did Nikki. So since they didn't, they probably think they can trade her for something."

"Like what?" Indigo said.

"Like Nikki's phone," I said.

"Or me," Blackhawk said.

We looked at him.

"I shot the asshole in the leg. He's probably holding a little grudge."

"Just a little one," Indigo said.

"Yeah, I can see that," I said. "Stake her out like a goat, wait till the tiger comes along and shoot him. So the other option is we sit here and wait for him to dangle the bait."

Blackhawk shook his head. "Rules of engagement. Never let the enemy choose the battlefield."

"So we attack while he's thinking up some grand strategy."

Blackhawk nodded. He looked at me. "Okay, we go. When?"

"We need to rest," I said. "Strip joints get busiest when guys get off work."

"If that's where he's at."

"That's where he's at," I said.

Blackhawk nodded. He turned to Jimmy. "You go on home. Come back tonight and open like nothing ever happened." He turned away, then turned back. "Get someone to patch the ceiling."

He looked at Nacho. "Be back at six." Nacho followed Jimmy out the door.

I looked at Indigo. "You crash here on the couch. I'll crash in the apartment."

"You leave that little girl alone," Indigo said with a grin.

"Get some rest," Blackhawk said, standing.

15

I called Pete Dunn and told him what I needed. Pete was my neighbor in the *Thirteen Episodes*. Since leaving Hollywood in the rear-view mirror, Pete was writing the great American novel. Which meant he spent a lot of time bored, staring out across the water. He had jumped at the chance to help me in the past. He jumped again this time.

We needed the layout of the Bush Club. Indigo was a pro, but she was a woman and women didn't usually go into strip clubs alone. At least without being noticed. She needed a date. So, before I fell asleep, I called Pete.

I slept for about four hours on Blackhawk's couch. I was awakened by Simone quietly shutting the door behind her. I sat up and slipped my shoe and my prosthetic on. It always took longer than I liked. By the time I stepped out on the balcony, Simone was at the bottom of the stairs. She went to the bar and poured herself a drink. I couldn't see what it was. She pulled herself up on a barstool. There was a slight movement across the room and I saw Blackhawk sitting on Elena's bandstand. Simone didn't appear to notice. I went on down.

I sat beside Simone. She didn't look at me. She had a water glass half full of brown liquid. Hair of the dog.

Big dog.

Without looking at me she said, "Nikki's dead." It wasn't a question.

Not a question, and no answer. Blackhawk stood and went behind the bar. He came around and stood in front of Simone.

"Have you ever been to the North Woods Bush Club?" he asked gently. Like he didn't want to startle her.

She took a healthy drink and almost gagged. She wiped her mouth. She shook her head. "Never heard of it."

Blackhawk studied her for a long moment. He looked at me. "She's a liability."

She leaned back, alarmed.

I touched her arm. "Relax, no one is going to harm you."

Blackhawk kept looking at her, making up his mind. Finally, he said, "Wait here, I'll be right back." He went around the end of the bar and walked to the stairs. He went up two at a time.

Simone twisted to watch him. She looked at me. "What is he doing?"

"He's anxious for Elena," I said. "He's never been good at waiting. Things are likely to get very ugly, very soon. He's figuring out how to keep you safe."

She took another big drink.

"Slow down on that stuff. You need to have your shit together today."

She looked at me like she was going to tell me to fuck off,

but then, she didn't. She set the glass down. She put her arms on the bar and laid her head on them. She began to cry. "What am I going to do?" she said in a muffled voice.

I didn't have the answer. I sat there like a bump. Jackson, the great comforter of women.

In a few moments, Blackhawk came back down. He sat on the stool next to her.

"How big is Luis's organization?" he asked.

She raised her head, gathering herself. "It ain't Luis's," she said. "He's just one of many guys that run things. There are guys like him all over. From here to California, and north into Oregon and Washington. From what Nikki told me, there's an outfit in California that runs it all."

Blackhawk thought about it. "So, they have people everywhere?"

She nodded.

Blackhawk looked at me. "She is not safe here."

She looked like she would cry again.

He reached into his jacket and pulled out a stuffed envelope. He laid it on the bar.

"There are five thousand dollars in here," he said. "I've called a driver for you. Go to the airport. Get on the first flight you find that is heading east. It doesn't matter where. When you land, check into a cheap motel. Change your looks. Color your hair, comb it different. Wear glasses. Get clothes you would never wear. Get them one size too large. Tomorrow, find a used car lot, buy the cheapest car they have. Pay with cash. Flip a coin to choose which direction to go, then drive the heap till it breaks down. Start a new life."

"I can't pay you back," she said.

"One day you will. Now, listen carefully, I'm going to give you a phone number." He told her then made her repeat it three times. "When you get to where you decide to light, you call the number. Tell them you are a friend of mine. They will help you get a new identity."

"Why would they help?" she said.

"Because Blackhawk is asking," I said. I looked at Blackhawk, raising my eyebrows.

"Echo," he said. Yeah, Echo was the paper guy.

She looked at me, then back to Blackhawk. "Who are you guys?"

"You don't want to know," I said.

She looked at me.

"No, I mean it," I said. "You don't want to know."

Pete Dunn came through the double doors. "There's a driver out front. Says he's supposed to pick someone up at this address."

Blackhawk stepped down and took Simone's elbow. She slipped off the stool.

"I don't have anything," she protested.

"Buy what you need at the airport. Tomorrow when you wake up in whatever city you land in, you can go shopping."

She looked back at me.

"Time to go," Blackhawk said. She threw her arms around his neck. She held on tight, then released him, turned and went out the door.

"Was that my date?" Pete said.

"Afraid not," I said.

He came over and sat beside me. "So, I'm supposed to be somebody's arm candy?"

I looked up and Indigo was coming down the stairs. Indigo with long, full, hair extensions, new eyelashes and a tight-fitting dress. She was carrying an overnight bag.

"Here's your date," I said.

He turned to look. His eyebrows went up. "Wow," he said. "Now that's arm candy."

16

Blackhawk gave Pete the keys to his Jaguar. I knew it hurt, but he did it. It was seven in the evening, and Pete and Indigo had taken the Jag and drove to the North American Bush Club. Nacho, Blackhawk and I had filled a shipping trunk with what we might need. Blackhawk kept a locked storeroom filled with tools of our old trade. Much like my rented storage locker out by the lake. We piled in Nacho's Jeep and headed for the club.

We parked two blocks away, rolled down the windows and settled in to wait. The Jag was nowhere in sight, so Pete had parked in the lot behind the club. We were closer behind them than I thought. We watched as they came strolling around the building and to the main entrance.

"Betcha they don't charge them a cover," Nacho said.

There were two beefcakes standing by the entrance. One of them had been collecting the cover charge.

"Why not?" I said, even though I knew the answer.

"They never charge good looking women. The more girls in the joint, the more men will show up."

"What about ugly women?" Blackhawk said. "Like five feet tall, five feet wide with hair in their ears?"

I was in the back, looking at him. He didn't even smile.

Nacho shifted sideways to look at Blackhawk. "Ugly girls don't come to a place like this," he said. Nacho took most comments seriously.

He settled back, looking at the two bouncers. "I think I know one of those guys," he said. "I worked with him back in the day."

Blackhawk turned and looked at me. "Does that change things?"

I shook my head. "Not much." I leaned forward to speak to Nacho. "When we go in, you advise your old friend that he might want to take a walk."

"I can do that," Nacho said.

It was an hour before Indigo and Pete came back out. The sun was disappearing, and the street-lights were coming on. The two bouncers spoke to them, wishing them a good day, and they walked around the building to the Jaguar. A minute later they pulled out, then went by us. Pete drove for a block then did a U-turn. They came up behind us. We got out as they did. Nacho moved around and popped the deck lid.

"What'd you find?" I said.

Indigo had the overnight bag. She set it in the back of the Jeep. She opened it, pulling the extensions out of her hair. She put the extensions in the bag as she pulled out a pair of jeans and a pair of Reeboks. In an easy movement, she pulled her dress over her head, completely unmindful that she was on a street, surrounded by men. Just one of the guys. She stepped into the jeans, pulled a tee shirt over her sports bra and sat on the tailgate, putting the shoes on.

"Strip joint upstairs, ground level," she said, tying the shoes. "Just the two guys out front. There are two bartenders inside, guy and a girl. When I tried to go downstairs, pretending I was looking for the lady's room, I got stopped. The guy that stopped me had pistol on his hip, covered by a sport coat. I know there were more guys downstairs, but I couldn't really see much. No Elena, but she has to be there. Why else would they have armed guards?"

"Cameras?" I said.

"Two outside front," she halfway pointed. "You can see them on each side of the door. Another one in the back corner covering the parking lot. Pointed the other way, so we don't need to worry about it. Inside, one in each corner, one over the cash register."

Blackhawk nodded at me, then opened the shipping trunk. He handed the Mossberg to Nacho along with a box of shells. Nacho shook them out and filled his pockets. Blackhawk gave Indigo her Berretta. I had my .45 Kahr in a hip holster and the Ruger LCP in an ankle holster. Pete stood aside, watching.

We had all dressed alike. Blue jeans, black tee shirts, running shoes. I reached to the back and pulled out a stack of broad brimmed straw hats I gave one to each of us except Pete. These hats were common in Phoenix. Especially in the summer. Anybody working out in the Arizona sun wore them. Of course, strip joints don't let hats inside. So ordinarily the hats wouldn't make it past the two bouncers.

"Never could understand why they don't let you wear a hat into a strip joint." Pete said reading my mind.

"Assholes go in there and put their hats on their laps and," he paused, looking at Indigo, "uh, abuse themselves."

Indigo laughed. "Jesus. Guys are just creeps."

I had cut a hole in the crown of each hat. I handed cans of black spray paint to everyone. "Let's do it," I said.

"What about me?" Pete said.

"You stay here and facilitate our tactical retreat," I said, without smiling.

"Facilitate? Tactical?" Indigo said. "You're a hoot."

"Come on," Blackhawk said and started toward the club. Halfway there he let Nacho take the lead. Nacho moved easily, carrying the shotgun close to his side, away from the street. I know we looked goofy in the hats, but hey, no one would remember anything but the hats.

Nacho marched straight up to the bouncers. He pulled up the brim of his hat, so they could see his face. He brought the shotgun around. They saw his face and they saw the shotgun.

"I'm suggesting you boys take a walk," he said softly.

The guy to my left was big and muscular, just the type to scare the average joe. As he recognized Nacho, his eyes grew wide. The other guy was big enough, but not as muscular. He started to say something, but muscles took him by the arm.

"Hey Nacho," he said quickly. "Hey no problem." He pulled on the other guy, "Dude, we gotta go," he said. The other guy looked confused, but he went.

Blackhawk and I stepped under the cameras, lifting the hats. Keeping them between the camera lenses and our faces. We sprayed through the hole in the hats, coating the lenses with black paint. We went inside.

17

We went in fast. The door opened to a landing with four steps leading up to the main floor. On the same initial level, to the right was an opening that led to the steps to the lower level. The stairs curved downward, disappearing before they reached the bottom. We spread as we went in. A big burly customer with a long bushy beard stood up and said, "What the hell?" Nacho hit him with a short chop of the shotgun butt. The guy went backwards and fell flat. That was enough for the rest. They sat still.

Indigo and Blackhawk moved quickly to each corner of the room. Using the hats and the spray paint, they coated each camera. I watched the stairs to my right. I didn't worry about the downstairs hearing us; the music was so loud you could feel it like an overcoat. Not sure why it was so loud. Guess it made the girls look better. There were two girls dancing topless, one at each end of the long bar. Two other girls were serving drinks, working through the tables. They were topless also. They stood rooted, staring at Nacho. Nacho is a big and scary looking guy. Everyone was looking at him.

The thing about topless women is, if your mind isn't on sex, they just look like women. Profound, huh? Blackhawk probably didn't notice they were topless. I'll bet Nacho did.

When the cameras were disabled, Blackhawk motioned at the two bartenders to sit on the floor behind the bar. They slowly complied. Nacho backed up, filling the door. It was psychological. You want to leave, you have to go through me. No one wanted to leave. No one was moving. It wasn't just Nacho. It was also the shotgun. Shotguns make an awful mess.

There is a great gun debate in this country. My opinion is simple. Hunting and sport shooting aside, there is no need for a civilian to have an AR-15, or anything like it. It is of no purpose. It is designed to kill men. Not big game. Not rabbits. Men. I think that most men that insist on owning one are only trying for a bigger dick. You want home protection, get a shotgun. Nothing like it.

Blackhawk and Indigo moved over to me. I nodded. I turned and headed for the stairs. They followed. At the bottom, the stairs opened up into a large, wide room, much like the one upstairs. There was a bar, like upstairs, left over from previous times. Two men sat on stools in the middle. They had glasses of beer in front of them. Ten steps away their AR-15's leaned against the wall. Luis sat at the end of the bar, facing the stairs. He was engrossed in a laptop. He didn't hear us.

As we moved into the room, the men swiveled. One reached for his waist-band. I pointed the Kahr at him and he stopped. Luis looked up and turned to ice.

Behind, and to the side of Luis, was a door. Blackhawk went to it and opened it. As he did I could see furnishings, like a small apartment. I had Luis on my front sight, and Indigo had the other two. Indigo could shoot ticks off a dog.

Blackhawk stood in the doorway for what seemed like forever, then we heard…

"What the hell took you so long?"

Then Elena was in his arms.

They stood embracing. I finally said, "Reunion later, we gotta go."

Blackhawk shoved Elena toward me. "Take her, I got something to do." He turned to look at Luis. "I told you, you are a dead man," he said coldly.

"No!" Elena said. "No, Blackhawk," she said emphatically, "he is not worth it."

Blackhawk looked at her. "No man harms you and lives. He has killed one of the two girls. He sells children for sex. He is not a human."

"I don't care," Elena said. "You won't do this. He is a pig. No more than a pig. You are a man of substance. He may deserve to die, but I don't want you to dirty your hands. You kill him, you stoop to his level."

They stood, looking at each other.

"Take her out," I said.

Indigo pointed her Berretta at the two men. "You two, go this way," she waved the gun at the end of the bar opposite Luis; they moved. "Get down behind the bar. If your head pops up, I will blow it off." They both disappeared behind the bar.

"Go on," I said to Blackhawk. Elena took his arm and pulled him. He reluctantly followed her up the stairs.

Society has laws. Most laws are black and white. But right and wrong is not black and white. Justice can be blind. That's why the girl holding the scales has a blindfold. Society's laws are made to prevent chaos. Most laws are good. Thou shalt not covet thy neighbor's wife. Thou shalt not steal. And thou shalt not kill. But many a soldier has killed or been killed in the name of a just cause. In the name of liberty. Blackhawk, Indigo and I had been trained to take lives. Quickly, efficiently, ruthlessly. Always, we were told, for the good cause of Mother America. But on the streets, sometimes in society, the situation doesn't always meet the rule.

Luis was still frozen. I looked at Indigo. She was looking at me. I nodded, then turned and followed Blackhawk up the stairs.

The shot reverberated up the stairway before I reached the top. Then, there was another. Just to make sure.

Indigo had been correct the first time. Leaving Luis alive had been Blackhawk's mistake. And it had almost cost him Elena. A mistake now corrected.

18

A month had gone by. The heat decided it didn't care what the past norms had been. It wasn't ready to go. Some idiots don't believe man's actions affect global warming. They also believe the contrails are government poison, and the moon landing was manufactured in a Hollywood soundstage. If you ever meet these people, don't get into a discussion. You can't change a brick from being a brick.

Pete had gotten a call from an old friend and had gone to Hollywood to help flesh out a script. He said it was a Western. He didn't hold out much hope for it. He said to get a Western green-lighted was harder than scratching the middle of your back in church.

Indigo had decided to stick around. She moved in with Nacho. Nacho came to me, all mush mouth and bumbling, asking if she was my girl, because if she was he'd step back. I assured him she was all his. When he told Indigo I'd said it was okay, she hit him in the mouth just for asking me. He told me it hurt and loosened a tooth. He said that's about as close as he'd ever come to falling in love.

Blackhawk and Elena returned to normal. Somewhat. Elena was more on edge and wouldn't go out without someone with her. She had to have heard the gunshot reverberating up the staircase at the strip club, but she never mentioned it. Blackhawk increased the surveillance equipment around the El Patron adding cameras on the perimeter of the parking lot. He hired two more bouncers and let Duane go. Or Duane quit. Whatever, I never saw him again. The new guys were retired cops. Both had years of experience working South Phoenix. Elena had called Boyce and Boyce had got their names from Captain Mendoza. They were older, a little paunchy, but they still had that dead-eyed cop look that would freeze the pod on most men. And they both had permits to carry. Which they did. Their names were Ben and Danny. Ben a silver haired guy who looked like he had been desk bound before he retired. Danny was Hispanic with a head full of salt and pepper hair and a perpetual smile. Don't let the smile fool you.

The little fracas at the strip club never came to light. No one had reported men with guns and no gun fire and no dead body was never reported. The female bartender had called the cops, but by the time they got there the place was empty, with even the other bartender gone. She said there had been a fight but when it became known that the cops were on the way, the place cleared out.

Blackhawk and I had watched the news, even Fox, and saw nothing. Jimmy checked the online police reports and arrests. Nothing. After a week I called Detective First Grade

Boyce. I asked her to check if there had even been a report at the strip club. I told her Nacho had a problem with one the bouncers and he was worried there might be some push back. She called back. There had been a report of a disturbance but nothing else. No complaint filed. I was in the middle of asking her how she'd been, when she hung up.

Even before running into Indigo at the casino, I'd felt sluggish and a step behind. I'd wake up in the morning and just lie there. I had to kick myself in the ass. I went back to my exercise routine. Mostly swimming. Three times, out and back, to the no-wake buoy that was just shy of three hundred yards from the stern of the Tiger Lily. Then jogging three times up to the Mustang and back down the hill. I pulled two twenty-pound weights out of the storage locker and worked with them until I had a fine sheen of sweat. The weight-lifter guys loved to lie on their backs and hoist hundreds of pounds of dead weight. Great for building the pectoralis major, which you need if you want to pick up a Volkswagen. The resistance of the twenty pounders actually made me stronger while building up my quickness. Snap a jab to the nose of the weight lifter before the guy even knows you moved.

I began to enjoy my down time. A couple of early mornings each week, Old Eddie would bump his skiff against Tiger Lily's stern, and I would climb aboard and go with him to slay the stripers. I got a case of the domestics and polished all the wood on the boat. I polished the brass and mopped the galley. I vacuumed the black-out curtains. I washed all the bed-clothes in the stack washer and dryer.

Even the ones from the guest stateroom, where no one had been in a long while. I brought all the weapons down from the storage locker and cleaned and oiled each piece.

Online, I had found a thick paperback book that had every Western Elmore Leonard had ever written. Score! I spent the sunset hours on top with a flagon of Plymouth, a dash of bitters and Elmore.

But, even with reading the best Westerns ever written, with maybe, just maybe, the exception of Dorothy M. Johnson, I was getting restless. So tonight I put the book aside. I took a shower, put on an old comfortable pair of jeans and a white linen shirt. I slipped on a Teva sandal and fastened a boot onto my stub. The boot looked like one that would be fitted to a broken foot. When asked, that's what I said it was. A cast for a broken bone. I had a number of stories as to how it became broken.

I combed my hair straight back, and *whooee* I was ready for the dance. I closed up, set my hidden alarms and walked down to the bar. Going out on the town for me was thirty yards away.

Across the way, on Dock A, I saw a newcomer. A huge seventy-five-foot Bravada. It was a monster. Three decks high. Sleek and new. Had to be over a million for it. I could see people on the fly deck. Looked like the Tiger Lily could fit on the helicopter port. There was no helicopter. I wasn't that surprised to have such a rig on this lake. I knew there was a dealer for them in Tolleson, and you'd find several on Lake Powell.

I was hoping Eddie would be in the bar. He sometimes

bartended when Maureen was short-handed. No such luck. The bartender was new. A funny looking little guy, about five seven, completely bald, with a narrow misshapen head. Like mom had trouble getting him out. He was all in white. He looked like the mini-version of a James Bond villain.

The cavernous bar was empty except for a couple sitting across the room at one of the wide-open windows. A mild breeze came drifting through. I picked a stool in the middle of the bar and ordered a Dewers and soda, tall. I normally drink Ballantine's but I like Dewers with soda. Some scotches go better with club soda. Some are good by themselves. The guy brought the drink and set it in front of me, snatched up the twenty I had put on the bar, and brought my change. I left it on the bar.

I drank slowly. I was in no hurry. No place to go, no one to see. Just fine. As the sun went down, the light changed until it was dark out, with only the dock lights outside and the bar lights inside. About the time it got dark I began to hear distinctive party sounds. It seemed to be coming from Dock A.

The bartender, who told me his name was Bernard, brought me my third drink.

"Sounds like a party," I said, to have something to say.

"Oh, hell yeah," Bernard said. "Guy brought a brand new Bravada in here yesterday. Seventy-five-foot long. People have been coming all afternoon. They're just getting started. Have you seen it?"

"Yeah, I noticed it when I was coming in here."

He looked puzzled. If I'd come in from the front I

wouldn't have been able to see it.

"I'm on the Tiger Lily, at the end of C."

"Oh, yeah. You're Eddie's friend."

"I like to think so." He moved down the bar, wiping glasses with a white dish towel. I sipped my drink.

Now it was pitch black out and the party was in full roar, when Bernard brought me my fourth drink. I was just beginning to feel them.

"I have to close soon," he said, setting the drink in front of me. I nodded. This was to be my last one anyway.

Across the room, two girls came in through the door from the docks. They both wore bikinis. The designer hadn't wasted much fabric. They were young, blonde and brunette, and immediately reminded me of Simone and Nikki.

They were laughing, and it was apparent they were just a little tipsy.

"Do you have a bottle of Captain Morgan spiced rum?" the blonde called to Bernard.

"Let me check," he said, looking behind the bar.

"And Mr. Penny wants two cases of Modelo."

"Here it is," Bernard turned with the bottle in his hand. He came down to the girls. "But we don't carry Modelo. I have Corona."

"Whatever," the blonde said, taking the bottle.

Bernard went to the back and came back with two cases of Corona, struggling to carry both. He hitched them up on the bar.

"Mr. Penny says to charge it to his bill," The brunette said. "Can you carry those to the boat for us?"

"I can't leave the bar, sorry," Bernard said.

The girls looked at me. "You want to go to a party?"

"Hey, he's a cutie," the blonde girl said. "You like Captain Morgan spritzers?"

"Aye matey," I said sliding off the stool. "I can carry those for you." I looked at Bernard. "Keep the change."

"Good luck," he said.

"Better lucky than good," I said. I hefted up the two cases of beer and followed two very appealing rumps out the door.

19

I awoke at first light. This was my routine since I'd started the new exercise regime. This time I didn't want to. My head was a little fuzzy and my mouth was so dry I couldn't even muster spit. It took a fleet second to remember where I was. On a large air mattress on the top deck of the Caledonia, the triple decker Bravada party barge. Nestled in the crook of my arm was a tousle of dark hair. I remembered now. Sometime after midnight, I had started something with the blonde, Lindy, and now I woke up with the brunette who calls herself Dey. Said she was named after one of the Partridge Family. Both girls were making the best of their youth. Vivacious, happy to party, slender ripe bodies. Young girls are always pretty. But, in the wrong light, sometimes you got a glimpse of what they would look like when middle-aged. Very few women mastered aging. Okay, me too, but it was worse for women.

Except for my boot, we were both naked. She was turned toward me, her mouth open. A crust of something was on the corner of her mouth. The hair was down in front of her eyes. Her breath had a spicy smell.

The taste in my mouth didn't all come from a night of partying. I just didn't believe in being that randy lily-pad jumping bullfrog that was only out after the latest conquest. Maybe a remnant of the wisdom left me by my Momma when I was very young. I am not immune to the pleasures of the flesh. I enjoy them as much as the next guy. It is just that the pleasure should come with some responsibility. And the pleasure is always greater when shared with someone special.

On this bleak morning I suffered the old dilemma, how to extricate yourself. The old joke of waking up nestled with someone coyote ugly. So ugly the coyote would gnaw its own leg off so as to not wake them. But, this one was far from ugly. At the same time, I still had a large desire to be elsewhere.

I took a slow five minutes gently removing my arm. What I had going for me was she probably wouldn't wake up if I started playing the tuba. Several Captain Morgan spritzers had gone into that tight little body. She probably wouldn't wake up until the sun began to broil her. I slowly sat up and heard a low moan at my back. I froze. I cranked my head around to see Lindy in all her glory. Her head was cradled in her arms, taking up what was left of the mattress. I was blank as to why she was there. A bad time for alcohol memory loss.

As delicately as possible I got myself off the mattress. I stood, feeling very exposed. We weren't alone. There were chaise lounges filled with sleeping party-goers lining both sides of the top deck. I spotted my trousers and slipped into them. My underwear and shirt were nowhere to be found. My Teva was about fifteen feet away. I slipped it on and made my way quietly down the gangway to the bow deck. Bodies of partiers were everywhere. It had been a bull bitch of a party. The big boat didn't even rock when I stepped off.

I stepped onto the Tiger Lily and reset the alarms. I went in, cranked the air up and drank a quart of water. I decided another hour's sleep wouldn't hurt, so I fell face down on the bed. I still had my Tevas on. But not my underwear.

I slept longer than I intended. When I finally rolled over and opened my eyes, I had a small, dull, throbbing between my eyes. I swung my legs over and stood up, then sat back down. The motion had caused the small throbbing to become a hammer. I took some deep breaths, then stood and went to the galley. I drank another quart of water.

Only one sure cure for this. I stripped out of the linen trousers and tossed them into the dirty clothes hamper. Without the underwear, a couple of memories came sliding back. I slipped my trunks on, fastened my swim foot and knifed the water off the back. I swam out to the buoy, treading water beside it, without holding on. I took several deep breaths, then swam back. I repeated two more times. The last time I got to the buoy, I held on. There is a remarkable perspective of the lake from that spot.

I was gazing out across the lake when something made me turn my head. The Caledonia had cleared her slip and was slowly moving past me, out of the harbor. The top was lined with party goers, somewhat recovered. I swung around to get behind the buoy. I sneaked a peek, and sure enough the two girls were side by side, in the middle of the crowd at the rail. I ducked behind the buoy again. I know, I know, it sounds as foolish as I felt. When I was dumb enough to take another peek, someone on the boat yelled, "Hey! There's someone swimming out there!"

I put my face in the water and swam like Michael Phelps in the last lap. When I pulled myself up on my diving stairs, the Caledonia was regally moving out into the middle of the vast lake. Well, I had wanted to go out on the town. I'd been in small towns that had less people than that boat.

I showered, slipped dry trunks on, changed my foot and found myself ravenous. I fixed a five egg, cheese and mushroom omelet. I toasted two pieces of wheat bread and browned two hash brown patties I keep frozen. A big glass of tomato juice and a pot of coffee. I slowly became human.

After cleaning the galley, I took the last of the coffee, Elmore's book and got comfortable on the back deck. The sun was warming the air nicely. I read a few pages, then nodded off. I jerked awake and read a few more pages before nodding off again. The routine was exhausting. This last time I nodded off, I was awakened by my phone. I had placed it beside me even though I had no earthly expectation of anyone calling me.

It was a text from Boyce. It said, "Do you know her?" There was a headshot of a woman with her eyes closed. I tapped it and enlarged it. I was awake now. It was Simone. She didn't look good.

I texted back, "Should I?"

She texted back, "Don't be an asshole. She had a matchbook from the El Patron in her back pocket."

I sat and stared at the photo, thinking about what to do when she texted again. "I'm on the deck in front of your boat."

I shook my head and sighed. I went through the boat to let her in.

She was wearing her normal kick ass cop attire. Dark hair back in a pony tail, dark tailored jacket over a crisp white shirt, opened at the neck. Dark slacks with a badge prominent on her belt just in front of her holstered pistol. The shoes were practical. Which meant, rubber soles that could race a gazelle.

"Come on in," I said sliding the double doors open.

She brushed by me and went to the galley counter and pulled herself up on one of the stools. She pulled a pack of cigarettes and a lighter.

"Mind if I smoke?"

"Yes," I said, leaving the door open.

She lit the cigarette and blew the smoke at me. "At least I asked."

I just shook my head and sat on the long yellow couch. No one in the entire world could get under my skin as quickly as Boyce.

"You know the girl, don't you?"

I just looked at her.

She looked back.

At last she said, "We have surveillance video of you and her at the same casino at the same time. We have the packet of matches found on her from El Patron. You've heard of the El Patron, haven't you?"

I just looked at her.

She slipped off the stool and went around the counter to the sink. She doused her cigarette under the faucet. She threw it into the garbage under the sink. She was well familiar with my boat. She had spent months on it convalescing from a gunshot wound.

She looked at me, "I love it when you sit, shaking your head like that."

I didn't realize I was shaking my head. I stopped.

She walked to the door. "I'm actually here to extend Captain Mendoza's invitation to join him at headquarters at two this afternoon. Knowing your supposed inabilities with modern technology I decided to deliver the invitation personally."

I stood. I think I was shaking my head again.

"Don't be late," she said. She turned and walked out into the sunlight.

20

I parked the Mustang in a no parking zone. It was five until two. I stepped off the elevator and started toward his office. Captain Mendoza had been promoted to the corner office. Along the wall to his left were three other offices, including the one he had occupied as a lieutenant. A sandy-haired guy was in that one. The rest of the huge room was filled with industrial styled grey metal desks with secretarial chairs. A third of them were filled.

I could see him through his plexi-glass. He was seated at his desk, engrossed in some paperwork. As always, he was immaculate. Dark glossy hair cut military style, the scalp shining through. Crisp white shirt with a maroon tie and a tie clip. His shirt sleeves sported golden cuff links. I could see his jacket hung neatly on a clothes hanger on a hat rack. He didn't have the hat rack before, so he had really come up in the world.

His door was open, so I walked in. He didn't look up. After a hesitation, I sat in one of the two chairs that fronted his desk. He still didn't look up.

When he did, I gave him my happy face with my eyebrows raised and a big grin. He just looked at me. He finally shook his head.

"Do you always have to play the idiot?"

I dropped the face. "My dad always told me to have a happy countenance."

He leaned back, looking at me. "Who was your dad?"

I shrugged. "I don't remember."

"But he told you what you just said?"

I shrugged again. "Not really. I don't remember much of what my dad told me. So, I just say my dad used to say this, or my dad used to say that. But, it's mostly what I say. I just don't want to appear to be a know-it-all."

"No risk there," he said.

He leaned down and opened a drawer. He rummaged for a minute, then pulled an 8x10 glossy print of Simone out and slid it in front of me. I looked at it. It was a glamour head shot. A lot of eye make-up. Her white blonde hair back lit for the halo effect. Seductive smile. I didn't pick it up.

I looked at the photo for a long time. Mendoza's eyes stayed on me.

"I'm told that you and she are acquainted."

"Were acquainted," I said. "Boyce sent me a text with her picture. She sure looked dead."

Mendoza nodded, "She is, .22 caliber to the back of the head. Homeless guy dumpster diving found her out by Metrocenter. No other signs of trauma. Nothing at the scene. No casings, nothing. Just a matchbook from El Patron."

"Sounds pro," I said. "The 22, not the matchbook."

He was still looking at me, in that cold, still, disconcerting way of his.

"We ran her through the system. Her name is Emily Sykes. Mother died when she was thirteen, leaving her with a stepdad. Ran away from home. He filed a missing person but didn't follow up. Ended up in L.A., working the streets. She was arrested a few times, so we have the prints. Then someone recruited her and turned her into a high-class hooker."

"Julie," I said.

He leaned back. "Julie," he repeated. "Why don't you tell me what you know."

"Boyce said there was video of me and Simone at a casino together."

He thought about it, then nodded. "Yeah, rival gangs went gambling at the same time and there was a fight. Boyce was watching the surveillance tape and saw you. And you and your friend appeared to be following a girl with white blonde hair. When the girl showed up dead, she remembered the hair. The camera by the elevators got a full face of her. Same girl. Why were you following her?"

Now I thought about it, I couldn't think of a reason not to tell him. At least most of it.

"Tomas Marino is the casino manager. He hired Blackhawk to help him with some unexplained losses his slots were taking. I came along for the ride."

"He's a casino manager and he doesn't know about EMP jammers?"

"Oh, I'm sure he does. I think he was sucking up to Blackhawk, trying to get Elena to perform for the casino."

For the first time I could remember, Mendoza smiled. "She's that good?"

"Oh yeah," I said. "She's that good."

"What's that got to do with the blonde?"

"Blackhawk and I were sitting there playing the slots when the blonde picked my pocket. I wanted my wallet back."

He studied me. "You let her pick your pocket."

I shrugged. "She was pretty good."

"But you let her."

I shrugged.

"Tell me about it."

So I told him. At least most of it. I told him about Simone and Nikki. I told him about Indigo but didn't get into how Blackhawk and I knew her. She was just friends with the other two. I told him that they were frightened and were running. I didn't mention Luis and the two men we shot. Imagine me not telling that? I also didn't tell him that Blackhawk had given Simone five thousand dollars to get out of town. Which she obviously had not done. She had tried to go back to her old life and had gotten herself killed for it. I was going to have to talk to Blackhawk about his philanthropic tendencies.

I told Mendoza about taking the frightened girls to El Patron. Then, that Nikki and Simone had just disappeared. We figured they had gotten what they wanted, and had moved on down the road. I did tell him that Indigo and

Nacho had hooked up. He almost smiled again.

He had me describe Nikki and Indigo. When I finished, he sat back, looking out across the room, deep in thought.

"Tell me what you know," I said. "Quid pro quo."

He swiveled back to me. "We didn't know about Nikki, or whatever her real name would be. We don't know about the woman, Indigo, but there are hundreds of them in that ring. We know about Julie."

"According to Simone and Nikki, Indigo was just someone they had met who was letting them stay in her room at the casino," I said.

"There is no record of any of them checking in or out of the casino hotel."

I just shrugged.

He looked at me. "We are working with California, Nevada and New Mexico. Emily Sykes was just one of, like I said, several hundred prostitutes working for the same large outfit. Julie is one of their recruiters. In fact, she's more than that. She's pretty high up in the organization."

I nodded.

"The Phoenix, Tucson, Flagstaff area is run by a guy named Luis. Luis Portofino. He unfortunately has gone underground. Did they talk about him?"

"Just to say a guy named Luis was the local boss. If you know all this, why not arrest them?"

"We will. We want to cut the head off the snake. We think the head of the snake is in Vegas, but he might be in California. Whoever it is, is really insulated. The top people are very careful. We're about there." He stood. It was time for me to go. "If you hear anything, I'll expect you to tell me."

Nothing to say to that.

21

As usually happens, the wind was up this afternoon. Tiger Lily was straining at her moorings. I had to collect the chaise lounge cushions and put them in their locker. The white-caps were ferocious. No one was on the water. It had been a cool and glorious morning. Feeling ambitious, I swam across the bay and back. I packed a bowl of cheerios with strawberries, blueberries and a banana, munched it while I drank a pot of coffee. I was reading Merle Miller's biography of Harry Truman. A president that was truly underestimated. I was always amazed that Roosevelt had chosen him to join the ticket his last time around. Surely the President was self-aware enough to know his health was fragile, at best. I guess we all feel immortal. Turned out to be a pretty good choice. I guess ol' Franklin knew more than the rest of us.

It's a lucky thing when you get to hand pick your partner. Blackhawk and I were thrown together, along with eight others. We didn't get the choice. But we were lucky anyway. I found that out during a ten-mile run. The colonel had chosen ten miles of extremely rough terrain, parts straight up or straight down, some of it through almost impenetrable forest. All ten of us had to finish or everyone started over. And we were on the clock. Three quarters of the way through, and cocky as hell, I turned my ankle. Blackhawk stopped, turned back and put me on his back. We made it on time. I didn't even know his code name at the time. But from then on, we were a team.

I usually read outside, but the wind was being unfriendly. It pushed me inside. I put a mix of old country female singers on and tried to get back into old Harry. After a while I was just dozing.

I snapped awake when the low throated bong sounded, announcing someone stepping onto the bow. I had the side curtains opened for light, but the blackout across the French doors of the bow were pulled. I gently moved one and through the crack could see Diesel standing, wagging his tail. There was a girl child petting him. I don't know which one had set the alarm off.

The girl was in the six or seven range, slender and beautiful with long blonde hair. She wore a light-yellow summer dress that was whipping in the wind. My first thought was she must be a guest of someone moored to my dock. I pulled the curtain back and opened the door. Now I could see a woman standing on the dock. Old enough to be the mother, but still young and pretty. She also wore a summer dress, printed with rose colored flowers. She leaned slightly, holding a fist-full of it to keep herself respectable in the wind. Beside her was a small duffle bag. She looked familiar, but I couldn't place her.

"Hi," I said. Diesel was sniffing at the girl, and she pulled back. "Don't worry about old Diesel, he's about as friendly as a dog can get."

"Honey, come up off the man's boat," the woman said.

"That's okay," I said, as Diesel began licking the girl's hand. "I think Diesel likes her."

The woman looked at me. "The guy at the bar down there," she looked back at the marina. "He told me how to find you. Do you mind if we come inside, out of the wind?"

I was puzzled, but I was taught to be polite, especially to ladies. "Sure, come on aboard."

The little girl stepped in, turning to the dog. "Come on, doggie."

Diesel just looked at her, then stepped off the boat and moved past the woman, down the dock. On to other pursuits. The woman picked up the blue duffel and stepped aboard. I reached forward and took her arm. She cautiously stepped into the salon. The girl had sat on the yellow couch. I waved the woman to sit beside her. I turned a galley stool around and perched on it.

The woman was looking at her hands. She had blonde hair, like her daughter. I assumed it was her daughter. They sure looked alike. She was a pretty woman, but not necessarily a striking looking woman. She was medium height. Despite having a daughter that age, she still had a girl's figure. She wore no makeup that I could tell, but still looked good. Makeup is overrated.

She looked up at me and stared at me. Her eyes were gray

green with small flecks of gold. I wouldn't know that until later when I had a chance to inspect her more closely.

"So, who was it told you how to find me?"

"The bartender guy. The funny looking one. Bald, short."

"Bernard?"

"Don't know his name."

"Yeah, Bernard. Why are you looking for me?"

She shifted nervously, then with sudden determination leaned forward and looked at me. "You don't remember me, do you?"

I was probably shaking my head, like Boyce says I do.

"You look differently in the daylight too," she said.

This time I purposely shook my head. "You've got to help me here."

"I know it was dark, and there were a lot of other people, but I would think you would remember me."

Dark and people?

Then it came.

"Lindy and Dey?"

She nodded.

"Where's Dey?"

"She followed the perpetual party up to Powell." She looked at her daughter who had picked up one of my True West magazines and was looking through it. "I've got Ashley, so that night was a one off for me."

Some of the memories made me slightly uncomfortable. Especially with the little girl sitting there.

"Can I offer you something to drink?" I said to cover up. Hell, I'm an adult and so is she. Don't know why I am slightly uncomfortable? I moved into the galley and opened the oversized frig. "I've got beer. I've got orange juice. I've got milk."

Lindy looked at her daughter, "Ashley honey, would you like some orange juice?"

The girl looked up. "Sure."

"Sure, what?"

The girl looked at me. "Sure, please."

"Coming right up," I said, glad to be doing something. I poured the juice, popped the cap on two Dos Equis and handed Lindy one.

Ashley took the glass with two hands and drank half of it. She set the glass on the coffee table and picked up the magazine. She had a sheen of wet across her top lip.

Lindy took a drink. I did too. She looked at me over the top the bottle.

"So, about now you are probably petrified that we have come knocking on your door."

I smiled. "Not petrified, but curious."

She nodded. "So, what it is, is this is a huge city and yet when the perpetual party left for Powell, you are the one and only person I know here."

"You don't know me."

She set the bottle on the carpet. "Yes, that is true." She looked at me, and her eyes welled up.

Well, shit!

"So this is something that only a truly desperate woman with a child would do," she said.

22

"Al Penny kicked me off the boat."

"Al Penny?"

"He's the guy that owns the Caledonia."

"Why would Al Penny who owns the Caledonia kick you off his boat?"

She looked around. "Do you have a television she could watch?"

I shook my head, "Nope. No television."

This information seemed to disappoint her.

"Do you like the magazine, honey?" she leaned toward the girl.

Ashley didn't look up. "It has horses in it."

"Mr. Jackson and I are going to go outside and talk a minute. I'll be right back."

This time Ashley looked up. I could swear her eyes looked old and tired. "Are you going to talk about my father?"

"You read your magazine, baby. I'll be just outside."

Ashley went back to her magazine.

Lindy looked at me. "Can we go somewhere to talk?"

I stood. "Out on the stern," I said. "And it's just Jackson."

Leaving her blue bag by the couch she followed me, giving one last glance to the girl before she stepped outside.

We were sheltered from the wind by the big bay cruiser in the next slip.

I leaned against the rail and waited. She stood, one hand on the rail, looking out across the lake. She appeared to need a moment to collect herself, so I gave it to her.

Finally, she turned and looked at me. "Eight years ago, I was involved with a guy. A very powerful, very rich guy. His name was Don. He developed projects in Vegas. Shopping centers, single housing communities. He developed Quail Run, the golf community. I was a realtor, and he hired me to show the model homes. I was young and single, he was older and married. He treated me very well. Put me up in one of the luxury houses. Took me on what he called business trips. But usually it was just a reason to go to some high dollar place and party. He really liked showing off his success, and I liked being a part of it."

She looked at me, almost defiantly, but her mouth twisted with pain, "In other words, Mr. Jackson, I prostituted myself to enjoy the good life. I didn't think a thing about it."

"Just Jackson," I said automatically. I could do the math. "But then Ashley came along."

She nodded her head, tearing again. "Yeah, and everything changed. As soon as he found out I was pregnant, he quit seeing me. He let me stay in the house, but I was never in the same room with him again."

I folded my arms across my chest. I've been told that is a physical defensive sign. Probably.

"This is very interesting, but what does it have to do with you seeking me out?"

"He left us alone. I worked as a realtor and Ashley grew up. It was really quite wonderful."

"But then?"

"His wife died. She got pancreatic cancer."

"And he wanted his daughter?"

She nodded. "I don't have any idea as to why. Up till then he hadn't given her the time of day. But then, I was getting her ready for school when I saw the car pull up in my drive. Two men got out. I know them both. They work for Don. They were always around, like bodyguards. As soon as I saw them I knew what they wanted. While they were ringing the front doorbell we went out the back. We walked about five blocks, and I called Uber. We went to the airport, and I had just enough cash to get us to Phoenix."

"No credit cards?"

"Just the one I used for work. A corporate card. I tried to use it, but he had it blocked."

"Where did Dey come in?"

"We worked in real estate together in Vegas. We were both big party girls back then. She moved to Phoenix, and we stayed in touch. I called her from Sky Harbor and she picked us up. We were staying with her when she asked me if I wanted to go to a party on a yacht. So we ended up on the Caledonia."

"We?"

"Al Penny had a stateroom with video games. Ashley was down there most of the time. I had put her to bed before you joined us."

I thought about us being on the top deck, and what we were doing. Good thing Ashley didn't have a midnight urge to come looking for Mommy.

"Just why did Al Penny kick you off his boat?"

"Because Dey has a big mouth. And the more she drinks, the bigger it gets. She told Al who I was, or more importantly, who Ashley was."

"Why should Al Penny care?"

"Because he, and everyone else, is scared shitless of Ashley's father. He didn't become a big shot developer on his own. He had some really powerful friends. It's well known his enemies end up in the desert."

"Mob?"

She nodded.

"And you knew this while you were with him?"

She nodded again.

"But why me?"

"Because I could tell you were a good guy. While all the other guys were flexing and bragging, you weren't. And, mostly, because the perpetual party is gone, Dey is gone with them and you are the only living human being I know in the State of Arizona. And I don't have a penny to my name."

"Not even Al," I said. She looked at me blankly. As usual my humor was lost.

Ashley appeared in the doorway.

"I'm hungry," she said.

Lindy looked at her and struggled with what to say.

I said, "Why don't we all go down to the marina and I'll buy lunch."

23

The bar was empty. Maureen, the manager, was tending the convenience store. I saw her in the store as I ushered Lindy and Ashley into the bar and seated them at one of the round high-tops.

"I'll be right back," I said and went to see Maureen.

She was stocking corn chips on the shelf. She was talking to herself as I came in. She was a stocky woman in her fifties, with gray streaked hair. She wore khaki cargo shorts and a pull-over golf shirt with the marina logo on it. He skin was brown and beginning to crepe up from years in the sun. She wore bright orange boat shoes. She loved her rowdy shoes.

I made a noise, so she would know I was walking in. She turned.

"Hey Jackson."

"Morning ma'am," I said.

She looked at me, "I told you about that ma'am shit. My mama gave me a name and you can use it."

"Yes mm….uh, Maureen. I've got a couple of ladies out there that are hungry. You suppose Bernard can rustle up some hamburgers?"

"The little shit had to go to the doctor. Why don't people get sick on their own time? If they can get to the doctor, they can work." She brushed her hair back. "I don't suppose you've seen Eddie around."

"Probably out fishing."

"Well, if you see him, tell him to come tend bar and there are some lightbulbs out on A dock." She turned back to stocking the chips. "You know where everything is. Fix your own burgers."

"Okay." I bit the ma'am off.

I went back to the girls.

"Guess what," I said. "We get to fix our own burgers." I looked at Ashley. "Would you like to help me cook? We get to have it our way."

Ashley perked up. "Can I, Mommy?"

Lindy smiled. "Sure you can."

"If you sit at the bar, you can watch," I said to Lindy.

They slid off their stools and Lindy mouthed "Thank you".

The kitchen area was separated from the bar room by a wall with a long, rectangular window, giving a long view of the kitchen.

Lindy slid up on a barstool, and Ashley followed me into the kitchen. The kitchen was pretty large. It had an oversized stainless-steel refrigerator. There was a matching freezer door that opened to the large cooler locker. Along the kitchen side of the window was a wide griddle. At the end were two deep fat fryers. Before he left Bernard had filled all the condiment trays. I fired the griddle, then opened the refrigerator and pulled three frozen hamburger patties. I handed them to Ashley.

"Okay, honey, hold on to these a minute so the griddle can get hot. Be careful not to touch the griddle, it'll burn your fingers, and that hurts like the dickens."

She took the burgers and stepped back from the griddle. I found the buns and went into the locker to find the sack of frozen French fries. When I found them I said, "You can put the burgers on now, honey."

She happily turned to comply. The burgers were separated by thin squares of paper. She put the burgers on the griddle, paper and all. I laughed, dropped fries into the fryer basket and grabbed a spatula to salvage the burgers.

"We need to take the paper off first, sweetie."

She looked at me, her eyes large. "You said to put them on."

I laughed again. "You are absolutely right. My bad. I should have told you."

She looked out at her mother. "He told me to, Mommy."

"It's okay, it's okay," Lindy said. "You're doing good."

Once the burgers were sizzling I let her turn them with the spatula. I handled the fries. Too much potential for disaster for her. Once the meat was ready and the buns were browning, I pulled the buns and helped her dress them.

Mom wanted no onions or mustard. Ashley didn't want tomatoes. I drug mine through the garden. We ended back at the round high-top. Lindy told Ashley it was the best hamburger she had ever eaten.

When we finished, I cleared the table, except for their

Cokes and my beer. I walked the dishes back to the kitchen and put them in the sink. Them that cooks, don't wash. I came and sat back down. Lindy was gazing out the window. Ashley was looking at me.

After a while the silence become cumbersome.

I looked at Ashley, debating. I finally decided that whatever this is, she was a part of it.

"So, I still don't know why you came to me."

Lindy turned to look at me. "I truly don't know. Except, like I said. You are the only one I know."

"And, like I said, you don't know me. I might be worse than what you are running from."

She was steady, looking at me. She slowly shook her head. "No, I don't believe that. Just watching you with Ashley, I know you are a good man."

I shrugged, uncomfortable, "I don't know what I can do for you. I can loan you a few bucks, if you need it."

"I may," she said simply. "I think right now, I need to be out of sight. I saw a spare bedroom, maybe you can put us up for the night?"

"Are we hiding from Daddy?" Ashley said, watching her mom.

Lindy looked down at the table, then at Ashley, "Baby, you don't even know your father. He says he's your father, but he sure as hell ain't your daddy."

Ashley's big blue eyes looked at me.

I looked out the window.

Sucker.

"Maybe just for the night," I said.

24

The wind had stopped, the sun was down, and Lindy and I were on the stern watching the light on the far mountains as the moon rose. The only sound was the soft lapping of the water against Tiger Lily's hull. We had spent the afternoon teaching Ashley card games which she had blatantly cheated at. The girl didn't like to lose. I tried to teach her checkers, but it was the same thing. She changed the rules, so she could jump sideways. This bothered her mother but tickled me. I've been known to change the rules and jump sideways. And the stakes had been considerably higher.

Ashley had showered in the oversized stall. She had been wrapped in one of my white tee shirts, in which she had delightfully paraded around. Her mother finally tucked her in bed. I was glad that I had that case of the domestics and had cleaned the stateroom.

I had fixed a scotch. Lindy was sipping a Dos Equis. I am a highly trained, world class, waiter, so I was waiting. The silence finally wore her down.

"You don't ask many questions," she said, without looking at me.

I shrugged.

"I really appreciate you letting us stay," she said.

I shrugged again.

She was silent for several minutes.

Finally, she said, "His name is Don Newman. You ever hear of him?"

I shook my head, "Nope."

"He's a big-shot in Vegas."

"So you said."

"It's funny," she said, "he never went to the strip. He really didn't like it. Said it was for suckers."

"Where did he go?"

She laughed. "Hey, a question." She took a drink, "He liked to go to Tahoe. Had a real mansion there. Five bedrooms. Giant great room with a stone fireplace that covered the entire wall. He'd fill the place with party girls, invited business types. Booze and food and a huge heated pool. Two large Jacuzzi's, hold twelve people. It would get naked and crazy at night. One side of the big room there were two poker tables, and they were always full, night and day."

"You join in the games?"

She shifted to look at me. "Would it bother you if I did?"

I smiled at her. "Not in the slightest." Then I was sorry I said it that way. Sounded a little harsh, like I didn't care about her. Which, so far, I didn't.

She took another sip. "The answer is no. I don't know if I would have. I'd played that scene before. Before he came along. But he didn't want me with anyone but him. I had to be careful. If I spent too much time even just talking with one of the other men, he'd get jealous. So I always played it cool."

"How about him?"

"What about him?"

"Was he exclusive to you?"

"Sometimes he'd tell me to go lie by the pool. That usually meant he would be entertaining another girl. But to answer your next question, no it didn't bother me. I usually knew which girl it would be, and it wasn't like I was in love, wanting to get married. I was just having fun. Hell, I usually felt sorry for the girl. Don was no stud. Five minutes and he was done."

I chuckled, but she couldn't see me.

"But when I missed my period, I knew the party was over. The funny thing is that I was on birth control. The label said it was 99% effective."

"So Ashley's a one percenter?"

"Yep."

I lifted my drink and looked at it.

"You're not drinking," she said.

I stood. I looked out over the lake. It was beautiful. I leaned forward and poured my drink overboard.

"I guess it's just not a drinking night," I said. "I think I'm going to hit the rack."

She looked up at me.

"See."

"See, what?"

"You're a good man."

I looked at her. The moonlight made her look very attractive, "What does that mean?"

She stood and moved her chaise over to the side, where it had been when we came out. "You're not even going to make a pass at me."

I didn't know what to say to that. She was right. It hadn't crossed my mind.

She stepped through the open door into my bedroom. "You have a big bookcase. You mind if I read awhile?"

"Help yourself," I said.

The sky had that grey, pre-dawn light when I awoke. Lindy had left the light over the sink on. For a nightlight I supposed. Their door was slightly ajar. I stood outside the door and listened to Lindy buzzing. I assumed it was Lindy.

I went back to my stateroom and slipped on my trunks, then put on my swim foot and goggles. I went carefully down the ladder and dropped silently into the water. It woke me up, as it always does. I felt ambitious this morning. I started for the shore, well past the buoy, on the other side of the opening to the marina bay. I dug into the water, slowing bringing my rhythm up until I was effortlessly slicing through the water. I kept my ears tuned for the sound of the early ambitious fisherman, rumbling out to seek that early morning bite. I could expect them, but they wouldn't expect me.

By the time I was back, hanging onto my ladder, I was sucking in deep gulps of oxygen. I waited until my heart rate came back to normal. Content to watch the silver morning mist rise from the deep water, with the golden morning light rising against the far maroon mountains. When I was back to normal, I kicked off and started another lap.

This time when I reached the ladder, Lindy was standing on the stern, wearing one of my tee shirts, drinking a cup of coffee. As I dog paddled I could smell it. It smelled delicious. She looked down at me, smiling.

"I found the coffee, hope you don't mind?"

"Not if I can have some too."

She turned away. "I'll get you a cup while you dry off. How do you like it?"

"Creamer and sweet and low," I said to her retreating back. In the unit I drank it black. I was getting soft. I hopped up the ladder and grabbed the oversized towel I had left on the chaise. I dried off, took the swim foot off, then stepped into the head, took a quick shower and brushed my teeth and hair. I slipped on dry trunks, my regular foot and a black tee shirt. When I came out, Lindy had a steaming cup of joe on the counter. The creamer and Sweet and Low were sitting beside the cup.

She was sitting at the counter, holding her cup with two hands. I could see Ashley on the bow feeding pieces of a bagel to Diesel. I doctored my coffee and joined her. She leaned back and looked at my foot.

"I remember now. You broke a bone in your foot. How do you swim with that thing on?"

I held my leg out and looked at the prosthetic. "It was a small lie. I don't have a foot."

Her eyebrows went up. "You don't have a foot?"

"That's what I said," I smiled.

"How did you lose your foot?"

I shrugged lightly. "When I was a kid I worked at a factory in Illinois. I got it caught in an open auger. Took it right off."

"Oh my God." she set her coffee down. It splashed over the rim. "That's awful."

"Didn't even hurt. Till later, that is. Hurt like the dickens later."

She got up and got a paper towel and swabbed the counter. "You sure handle it well. I couldn't even tell you had a problem."

"Lots of practice," I said.

I swiveled to watch Ashley and Diesel. Ashley was tossing pieces of bagel out on the dock. Diesel would jump off, grab the bagel and jump back on. The bagel piece lasted one gulp.

"That's as active as I've seen Diesel in a long time."

"She loves animals. Especially dogs. With her in daycare, and me working all day, a dog at the house didn't make any sense."

"Usually Diesel gets his exercise chasing gulls off the dock."

She sat back down. "Yeah, I saw those. How are there seagulls in the middle of Arizona?"

I smiled, "Easier than you think. From the ocean they follow the Colorado up to the Williams then follow the Williams to Alamo Lake. It's just a short hop from there to here. I've even seen pelicans at Alamo."

She smiled. "I don't know where Alamo is, but that's just weird."

She finished her coffee and went to the sink to rinse the cup. She placed the cup in the drain rack, and turned to look at me. She rested her back against the sink, each hand on the edge of the counter. She looked at me for a long moment. I could see she was making up her mind on something. So I let her.

Finally, she said, "I'm afraid I have to take you up on your offer."

"Oh?"

"For a few bucks, I mean. You said you could loan me a few bucks. I don't have any money, someday I will, and I'll pay you back. I promise. What we have is in the duffel, and it's not much. I need small stuff, like toiletries and feminine things."

"Sure," I said. I slid off the stool and went to my stateroom.

When I returned I handed her five bills. She took them and looked at me, her eyes larger.

"Five hundred dollars? I don't think I'll need that much."

"Buy what you need," I said. "You'll pay me back, I'm not worried. There is a Walmart at Noterra. It's right down the road on I-17. You can get everything you need there. Get some food too. I wasn't expecting company."

"You are going to let us stay?"

"Until we have a plan."

She put the bills in her pocket. "How am I going to get there?"

"I'll call a ride for you. The shuttle will take you up the hill. They'll meet you there. It is my personal app, so have them wait, I'll be charged."

She came to me and put her arms around me. She kissed me. A sisterly kiss.

I called for a ride and ten minutes later she had hugged Ashley and told her to be good for me. At the gate she turned and waved at us. She went through it. I watched the top of the hill until I saw her get into her ride.

She didn't come back.

25

I am not prepared to entertain a seven-year-old girl, so I was ecstatic when Eddie bumped his old skiff up against my stern. Eddie was the grizzled old marina handyman. Maureen let him earn the slip rent for his old river runner scow he lived on by doing the odd jobs around the marina. He'd been thirty years on the Chicago police force and was a fierce slayer of striped bass, crappie and just about any pan fish. If he wanted a special meal he caught the sleek, white bellied, channel cats. He also was very handy and could fix about anything. I'd used him for help more than once. Awhile back I'd helped him with a problem his nephew was having. We'd become close friends. He was a man, like me, that liked his alone time.

I had taken Ashley out on the docks and walked them, showing her the different boats, and the different birds. She had laughed gleefully when Diesel had rousted a flock of gulls, sending them screeching and crying into the sky. We went into the marina where I introduced her to Maureen, who smiled at the girl and looked at me suspiciously. She gave Ashley a candy bar.

By the time we were back on Tiger Lily, she had eaten the candy bar, with a healthy trace of it around her mouth. I had no little kid things for her to do. I had gone through all my books, trying to find one for a seven-year-old. Finally, in desperation I found my book of poems by Emily Dickinson. To my amazement she could read it. She was a good reader, well beyond her years. She told me her teacher always chose her to read to the class. I felt an odd sense of pride.

When Eddie bumped up against us, she was on the yellow couch with the book on her lap. I was sitting at the counter watching her. Her lips didn't even move. Sometimes she would read aloud to me.

I went to the back and opened the sliding stern doors. Eddie climbed up, dressed in his Eddie uniform. Khaki trousers, work boots and an old worn chambray shirt. On his head was a billed cap that had been sweated through so heavily that whatever it had been advertising was now indistinguishable.

"Figuring on heading up to Cottonwood Creek, they say the crappy are schoolin' up there. Thought you might like to come along?"

"I've got company right now."

He stepped back. "Oh, sorry. Don't mean to interrupt."

"Nothing like that," I said. "Come on, I want you to meet her." I turned, and he followed me into the main salon. Ashley was concentrating so hard she didn't notice us coming in.

"Ashley," I said. "I want you to meet a friend of mine."

She looked up.

"This is Mr…."

"Just Eddie," he said.

"This is Mr. Eddie," I finished.

"How do you do," Eddie said.

Ashley got shy and didn't know what to do.

I looked at Eddie. "Her mom's a friend. She's here for the day." Eddie just looked at me.

"Have you ever been fishing, Ashley?" I said.

Eddie smiled, turning back to the girl.

She looked at me.

"I'm afraid she's been raised a city girl," I said. I looked at Eddie. "Not too soon to start her education. You mind if she came along?"

"Never turn down a pretty girl."

She was watching me. "How would you like to take a boat ride with Mr. Eddie and me," I said to her. "Maybe we can try our hand at catching a fish. Do you know about fishing?"

"I'm not dumb," she said.

Eddie laughed out loud.

"Well, there you are." I looked at Eddie. "I don't think I have a pole to fit her pistol, do you?"

He nodded. "I think I have an old Zebco 202. I'll go get it and rig it up. Be back in half an hour."

He was right on his word. He pulled up a half hour later. Besides the pole, he had a brand-new life jacket. Kid sized.

He held it up to me. "Figured we'd need this. I went in

to buy it, but Maureen donated it. Said she'd put it on my account. On account she'll work my ass off to pay for it."

Ashley stuck her head out the door.

"Oops, sorry," Eddie said.

"I heard bad words before," Ashley said.

I shook my head. No doubt, little girl. No doubt.

A few minutes later we were trundling across the water. We didn't zip, we trundled. Eddie's old fishing dingy didn't zip anywhere. Ashley trailed her hand in the water. It was about as nice a day as you could ask for.

It took the better part of an hour to make our way to the area he wanted to fish. I sat beside her and explained the workings of a rod and reel. She was fascinated with the minnows he had in his bait bucket.

I told her that sometimes Eddie would throw a large seine net and catch lake shad to use for bait. I told her sometimes he used night crawlers or anchovies. She said "Eewh, I hate anchovies."

"Yeah, I don't care for them on my pizza either," I said above the noise of the motor. "But the fish love'm."

She looked at me. "If fish eat anchovies will they taste like anchovies?"

"Good question. Nope, they just taste like fish. Some better than others."

Eddie putted us into a small bay and began angling the boat back and forth. He leaned into his old Hummingbird depth finder. I didn't know anyone better at finding fish than this guy.

Finally, he said, "There they are."

He slid to rest forty feet straight off a point. When he got the skiff where he wanted it he cut the motor.

"Drop the anchor," he said to me.

I lifted the scarred blue anchor off the coil of rope and carefully dropped it in the water. I let the rope ease through my palms until it stopped.

"Give it a couple feet of loose," Eddie said. "That way it will drag instead of bounce."

I did as he said. "What if it gets snagged?"

He smiled at me, "That's why I bring you along. You can just swim down there and un-snag it."

Ashley looked at him wide eyed, then turned and looked at me and laughed. Eddie winked at her.

Ashley was a good study and listened intently as Eddie rigged her pole. She was almost on top of him, watching. I sat at the back watching this grizzled old man, seventy plus years of life etched across his face, and the pure smooth face of the child who had barely experienced any life yet. He went through the skilled motions of getting a minnow on the hook. She didn't flinch when Eddie showed her the exact place, behind the dorsal, to puncture the bait fish.

"If'n you go too far forward you kill the minnow, and crappie don't usually hit dead bait. Too far back and the minnow will get off. You got to do it just right."

He dropped the bait in the water.

"Another thing," he said. "Lookit this line here." He pulled the line toward him. "I've marked it every ten feet." He held it out for her to see. "See the dark spot on the line here? That's where I took a magic marker to it."

She was looking intently. She nodded her head.

"So," he continued, letting the line back into the water. "When that mark hits the water, you know the bait is ten feet down." He turned to the depth finder. "Now this here contraption tells us that them fish is forty to forty-five feet down. So, how many marks do we want to let down in the water, so the bait is at the right place?"

She just looked at him, not getting it.

I tried to help. "So, how many tens go into forty?" She looked blankly at me.

"Have you studied division and multiplication yet?"

She looked back at Eddie. She didn't shake her head in disgust, but it seemed like she did.

"I'm only in the second grade," she said, almost disdainfully, "but, you want three more of them marks to go down if you want to catch those fish."

26

Ashley squealed with delight when she caught her first fish. All told, we caught about thirty. When we putted back to the Tiger Lily it had been a good day. Halfway back Ashley put her head on a lifejacket and went to sleep.

Eddie insisted on doing the fish cleaning, so I roused Ashley, got her up the ladder and put her in her bed. I put on some low music and opened Elmore again. Two hours later she stumbled out of the stateroom, eyes heavy with sleep. The first thing she said was, "Where's Mommy?"

"She's been detained." I lied and felt guilty about it.

"Am I going to do another sleep-over?"

"Sure. We can play cards or play another game of checkers."

She looked at me with solemn eyes. "You're not very good at it."

"Maybe I just need more practice."

I had no idea what to do with this girl child. Finally, as the sun was dipping, we walked to the marina store, just before it closed. There was a teenager manning it. I bought

Ashley an ice cream bar. We found a box of crayons and a coloring book of exotic birds. Later I made some of my world-famous spaghetti and we went to bed early.

I was awake at first light. I was thinking about Lindy. It was obvious she was a loving and attentive mother so that meant her absence was probably not self-motivated. I couldn't see her just running off. So, where was she?

I decided to forego the swim this morning. I put the coffee on. When it was completed, I took the big mug out on the bow. Diesel was down at the end of B dock, lying in a patch of sun. Movement down by the store caught my eye. The marina provides showers for those that have been skiing or swimming and want to come into the bar. Eddie was coming out with a brightly colored towel around his neck. It was one of the few times I had seen him wearing shorts. His legs were skinny and white. He saw me and raised a hand. I lifted my cup.

He decided to join me. He came through the gate and made his way to me. As he did, I went in and poured another cup of coffee. I peeked in at Ashley. She was still down and out. I brought the coffee out. Carrying both cups, I stepped off the boat onto the dock.

"She's still sleeping, let's sit on Pete's," I said softly. I took the cup and we walked down to the Thirteen Episodes. We stepped aboard, pulled the chair covers off and sat.

"Lindy's not back yet," I said.

He looked at me, taking a sip of the coffee. "Lindy's the mom?"

I nodded. He didn't say anything more. Eddie was a

private man and gave others the same respect. He wouldn't pry. He figured if you wanted him to know something, you'd tell him. So, I told him. Told him how I'd met Lindy, how the two of them had come to me, and why. Told him what Lindy had told me about Ashley's father.

He listened silently. I finished and leaned back. I was looking across at the Tiger Lily, looking for movement, any sign the girl was up.

After a long silence, he said, "What are you going to do if the woman doesn't come back/"

The sixty-four-thousand-dollar question. I shook my head. I had no answer.

We were silent again.

"Most folks would call CPS," he said, finally.

"Child Protective Services? You think that's a good idea?" I asked.

He shrugged. "Don't know. Experience I had in Chicago was some good, some bad. Screwed kids up being away from their parents. But, on the other hand, some people ain't fit to be parents."

"I think this one is a good mother."

"Girl should be with her mama," he said.

I nodded.

A small white face appeared at Tiger Lily's bow door. I stood up.

"Guess I'll go try to figure out what to do with a seven-year-old."

"I'm working the bar today," Eddie said.

I shook my head and smiled. "You did enough yesterday."

He stood. "I've got a dozen fillets I froze up for you. I'll bring'm down later."

"Appreciate it," I said. "No rush."

I replaced the chair cover and stepped off Pete's boat. I went down to the Tiger Lily, stepped aboard and through the sliding door. She was sitting on the yellow couch. Tears were running down both cheeks. I guess I should've been there when she woke up.

I sat beside her and put my arm around her. She leaned into me and began to sob.

"I want my mommy," she cried, her voice muffled against my side.

So do I, I thought.

I started talking. Anything to get her mind on something else. I talked about the fishing we had done with Eddie. I talked about how we needed to go shopping. I told her we needed to buy her some new clothes, and maybe get some books just for her. It took a while, but I finally jollied her into a smile. I got her busy with me in the galley making what I called Jackson's world-famous flap-jacks.

I laughed a little too hard when she asked, if they were world famous, how come she'd never heard of them.

After we ate, we cleaned up, caught a ride on the shuttle up the hill and drove to the Walmart. We spent an hour finding clothes and books, and another hour grocery shopping.

Back at the boat, I was putting everything away and she was reading on the couch when they came for her.

27

There were three of them. All dressed in business suits. I caught a glimpse of them coming down the dock. They walked single file. The lead man was big and blonde, with a florid face. The other two were darker, of medium height. It was warm, but they wore jackets.

I reached down and took the book from Ashley's hands. She looked up in surprise. I took her hand and pulled her up.

"I need you to do me a favor," I said, leading her through the galley. I took her to the bathroom with the oversized shower. "I need you to stay in here for a bit. Go ahead and read. You can sit on the toilet."

"I don't have to go," she said.

"That's okay," I said. "Just stay in here until I come to get you."

Her eyes were wide, but she stayed. I shut the door behind me.

I went down the hallway and out on the bow. I stepped out on the dock as they reached me.

"Boy, you Seventh Day Adventists are relentless," I said cheerily to the big guy. "But I already gave at the office."

He was puzzled.

"If you want to leave your pamphlets, I promise I'll read them."

He came to a stop, and the other two fanned out behind him. He was a lot bigger than I was. He didn't expect any trouble from me.

He looked at the boat and then to the guy on his right.

"This the right boat?"

The guy leaned down and looked at the side of the boat. "Tiger Lily," he said. "It's the right boat."

"Hate to disappoint, but she's not for sale," I said, wishing I'd snagged the Ruger on my way out.

"We come for the girl," the big guy said.

I stood looking at him, and it pissed him off.

He pulled the jacket to the side to show me the shoulder rig and the automatic in it. "Don't fuck with me, boy. Get the girl and we'll be on our way."

"Where's Lindy?"

"She sent us to get the girl."

"I'll give the girl to Lindy," I said.

"You'll give her to me," he said. "Get the girl."

"What are you? A fucking parrot? Get the girl, awwk, get the girl."

His florid face turned redder and he reached for me. He was probably used to just grabbing a guy and beating him to death with his big meaty fists. As his hand came to grab me, I turned it aside. This turned his shoulder slightly and I gave him a little shove. He took a step to steady himself. The damn fool forgot he was on a dock. His foot went out over empty space. While he thrashed, struggling for balance, I shoved him again. Just a little shove. He went over the side and made a spectacular splash.

I heard a high laugh and I turned to see Ashley on the bow. She had a big grin. The guy was thrashing in the water, trying to grab the dock, but the struts were coated with years of algae. Slick as snot. I wondered if he could swim.

Both of the other two began digging in their jackets for their pistols.

A big voice of command said, "Hold it!"

Ten paces down the dock, Eddie stood. He had a double-barreled shotgun leveled at the men. They froze. I discreetly stepped out of the line of fire.

I waved at Ashley, "Go back inside, honey." She just looked at me. "Go now!" I said harshly. She turned and went back inside.

The men stood, not moving, eyes on Eddie. The big guy was still thrashing in the water. Eddie looked at me. "Now what?" he said.

I looked at the two. "Turn and face the end of the dock," I said. They reluctantly complied. When they were turned, I said, "Take the guns out and lay them on the dock."

They did. They didn't want to, but they did. "Get the fuck off my dock," I said. "I give the girl to her mother. No one else, now go!"

They turned and hustled by Eddie. He had stepped on the bow of Thirteen Episodes to let them by. I kicked their guns into the water. I stepped aboard and reached down to open a locker. I pulled a life jacket out, stepped back onto the dock and walked over to the edge. I looked down. The big guy was struggling to hold on to one of the struts. He had his gun in his hand. He looked up at me, but he didn't point the pistol. I showed him the life jacket.

"Trade you the gun for the life jacket," I said. He looked at me like he didn't understand. "Throw the gun away and I give you the life jacket."

He looked at me for a long time, then finally tossed his gun. It landed with a plop. I dropped the life jacket down onto him.

"Now, get the fuck out of my lake," I said.

28

When Blackhawk showed up, he had Elena and Indigo with him. They each carried an overnight bag. As they stepped into the salon Blackhawk said, "We thought we'd take a boat ride."

I was looking at him. I had called and told him I could use a hand, and now the whole gang was here.

Ashley was lying on the couch reading. She slid her legs to the floor and stood up as they entered.

"Ashley, these are my very good friends, Blackhawk, Elena and Indigo," I said.

"Hi, Ashley," Blackhawk said. Elena gave her a bright smile. Indigo was watching me.

"Is that your real name?" Ashley said, looking at Blackhawk.

"Of course it is," Elena said. "My mamma named me Elena when I was first born. She named me after my great auntie."

Ashley got it. She grinned. "No, not you, him."

"His real name is Freddie Foobledorf," I said. Ashley

looked at me, then frowned.

"You're making that up," she said.

"Everyone calls me Blackhawk, and I would be pleased if you would call me Blackhawk," Blackhawk said. He put out his hand. "How do you do."

Ashley grinned at him and took his hand. She hadn't been taught to shake hands, so she wasn't sure what to do. Blackhawk shook her hand.

Indigo was watching me, and when I looked at her, she discreetly tilted her head to the stern. I looked back at Blackhawk. He was looking at me and nodded, as if in agreement.

He turned to Elena. "Can you show Ashley your new smart phone? Jackson, Indigo and I need to talk."

Elena looked at him for a moment, then put on a bright smile. She sat on the couch and Ashley sat next to her. "I have a new phone and you can watch movies and TV shows and all kinds of stuff. What's your favorite show?"

"I like the Barbie show, but Mom doesn't let me watch it. She says the girls are all mean to each other."

"Your mom's probably right," Elena said. "Here, let's see what we can find." She started fiddling with the device. I took that as our cue. Blackhawk and Indigo followed me to the stern. I quietly shut the sliding door behind me.

Indigo was looking around. "This is a piss poor place to defend," she said.

"I know," I said.

"Tell us about the girl," Blackhawk said. So I did.

"So the father sent his goons and one of them accidently fell in the lake?" Indigo grinned.

"Accidently," I said.

"What about Child Protective Services?" Blackhawk said.

"I like this girl," I said. "And the mother left her with me."

"So we stash her, and go find the mother," Indigo said.

"Easier to let the father find us, then we ask him where the mother is."

"Because he knows."

"Because he knows."

"Bad place to defend," Indigo said again. "Trapped here at the end of the dock."

Blackhawk was thinking, so I leaned against the rail and let him. Indigo was watching something out on the lake. I turned to look, and it was Eddie, way across by the dam, fishing in one of his favorite spots.

"You remember that cove where we spent a week, way down at the other end, by the river mouth. You and Boyce and Elena and me?"

I nodded.

"Who's Boyce?" Indigo said.

"Doesn't matter," I said. "Yeah, up close to the eagle preserve."

"That cove had only one way in, and the surrounding desert was too rugged and steep to traverse."

"If they find the boat gone, they'll know we're on the lake," Indigo said.

"That's true," I said. "But so what? They'll come for the girl. They think I'm some nitwit that got lucky bracing their muscle. And when they come, how are they going to come?"

Indigo smiled. Blackhawk was nodding, "In a boat," he said. "A tiny little boat, with them all bunched together. Out in the open."

"They could just wait us out," Indigo said.

"Too many places for us to go ashore. They don't have enough men to watch every ramp and every beach night and day. No, they'll come looking."

"We go now?" Indigo said.

"We need provisions. Probably for a week. I don't think they'll wait that long. You can bet the guy that went into the water wants his revenge."

Blackhawk said, "Okay, you and I go. Indigo stays with the girls." He looked at me. "I think we probably ought to stop at your storage unit."

29

It took over three hours before Blackhawk and I were back on the boat. I had picked where I lived because it was somewhat isolated and away from the city. Today was one of those rare days when I wished things were just a little closer.

The whole time we were gone, I was worried Newman and his boys might show up to take the girl. Blackhawk assured me that Indigo could handle them. And she could. I still worried. I was surprised I had taken such a proprietary attitude to this little girl. I wished her mother would show up.

We had gone back to Walmart and had stocked up with canned goods and beverages. Some adult. I bought stuff I thought a seven-year-old might like. I might had gone overboard. Blackhawk was much more practical. We also had stopped at my storage unit and filled the trunk with ammunition for all the pistols we carried, including rounds for Indigo's Berretta. I snagged the AR-15 with ammo, and two Mossberg 590 pump shotguns with four boxes of shells.

At the last minute I grabbed a flare gun with a half dozen loads. We loaded all the weapons in an oversized blue canvas duffel. It was heavy as hell.

When we carried all the stuff on board, Indigo was up top with binoculars, and the girls were on the couch watching Elena's phone. Elena extracted herself to help us put stuff away, but Ashley was too engrossed to even look up.

"What's she watching?" I said softly.

"I gave up," Elena said. "The mean girls."

Once everything was on board, I gave Blackhawk one of the Mossbergs and a box of shells. He had two clips for his Sig Sauer in his pocket. He took the keys to Swoop and went to get her. Swoop is my twenty-foot Grumman sport deck. It has an eight-foot beam and can do an easy forty miles per hour unless the wind and the waves are up. I keep it wet docked on the outside dock.

It took me an hour to swing the Tiger Lily to the dump station and empty the honey pot. Then back around to the gas dock to top off. Indigo sat in a chaise lounge with the binoculars on her lap. Maureen came out to gas me up.

I stood beside her as she handled the pump. She looked at me with a twinkle in her eye. "Heard some fella had a little accident down by your boat. Seems he fell into the water."

"Accidents happen," I said. She didn't look at me, but I could see she was chuckling.

"I'll be gone a few days," I said. "I don't want anyone to know where I am, but if Eddie needs to find me, I'll be up in Humbug Bay, by the eagle preserve."

"That's off limits," she said.

"That's the point," I said.

"Lake patrol will find you. You'll get a ticket."

"I won't go too far," I said. "Just this side of the line."

"Your funeral," she said, pulling the gas nozzle out and replacing it on the pump. "Want this on your tab?"

I nodded. "Appreciate it.'"

"Be safe," she said.

Blackhawk was sitting out on the water, bobbing and waiting. I went up top. Using the cockpit controls, I brought Tiger Lily away from the gas dock and out onto the main lake. The wind had come up and there were white-caps across the water. It was slow going. The Lily was a stately, wide old dame waddling slowly across the water, like the heavy old woman she was. Slow and steady, lifting her skirts to avoid the puddles.

I had lied to Maureen. We went into Humbug Bay and went past the posted signs until I found the cove we had remembered. As we entered, it opened up enough that I could back and fill until we were pointed back the way we came. It went far enough back from the main lake that anyone following us in would be in our sights long before they reached us. It was a crooked cove, so we couldn't be seen from the main lake. I had Indigo drop the stern anchor and I gently pulled up against it until we had used much of the thick anchor line attached to it. Then I had her drop the bow anchor and pulled back from it for about twenty feet. Then I reeled in the stern line until we were tight against both anchors. She wouldn't swing, even in the wind. If we had visitors I wanted her solid.

Blackhawk brought Swoop up behind us and putting the bumpers down, we fastened it snug to Tiger Lily. He climbed aboard. Ashley was still on the couch with the phone. Kids. A beautiful day out and she's watching something on a device. I shook my head. Somewhere along the line I had started thinking like a father.

Indigo came out of the head wearing a bikini. She lathered herself with sun lotion, grabbed the binoculars, a beer, and climbed the aft stairs. We were all going to take turns on look out. She was first.

I moved Ashley and Elena's phone out on the bow. At least she would get some sun. I pulled three bottles of beer and popped them, handing one each to Elena and Blackhawk.

Elena was watching me. "Blackhawk says you always know what you're doing," she said, taking a drink.

\ I sat at the counter. "Unless I'm on the dance floor."

She grinned, "Yeah, I saw that. That was pathetic."

"I only have one foot," I said.

"You have no rhythm," she said. "What I'm wondering is why you brought us here? To this place. Seems like we're trapped in here. Only one way in, and one way out. Don't seem smart. Those guys will find us eventually."

"Exactly," Blackhawk said.

"Exactly?"

"We're not hiding," I said. "If we were hiding we'd take Ashley out into the city. And, if they did find us there, we wouldn't know which way they would come at us."

"And here you know."

"Exactly. We want them to come to us. Remember, they think we are just civilians. Nobody to worry about. They don't know who Blackhawk is. They don't know who Indigo is or what she's capable of. They think the hardest part will be finding us. And they know we are on the lake. It's only a matter of time."

Elena looked at Blackhawk, shaking her head. "It almost ain't fair."

"Good," I said.

By the time it was late in the afternoon, we were all hot and stir crazy, so we went diapering. No, I'm not making this up. Experienced boaters know all about it. You take your life jacket and turn it upside down and step your feet through the arm holes. Now you have it on like a diaper. This allows you to bob around in the water, sitting comfortably holding your beverage, without the jacket riding up around your ears. Ashley loved it.

Blackhawk was up top, and Indigo joined us in the water. Just like it happens sometimes, seven-year-old emotions are hard to keep in check. One moment of playing and laughing, and then the next Ashley began to cry. Indigo and Elena immediately went to her. I was a little farther away, but I could hear the tone of their voices trying to soothe the girl. I was gratified that there was no edge between the women. That is not always the way.

Watching Ashley's sad face, I began to reevaluate my game plan. Maybe staying out here for so long wasn't a great idea. Maybe if they don't make a play, like tomorrow, we'll stash the girl and go find her mother.

30

Aware of the fragile nature of Ashley's emotions, everyone adopted just a little more of a jovial tone. As the sun disappeared behind the purple western mountains, and with the water becoming quiet and dark now, I laid out the silver space blanket on the bow. It protected the deck from the sparks of the small Smokey Joe charcoal grill. I fired the briquets up and set the draft for a nice hot set. Elena had Ashley helping her in the galley. They were prepping the vegetables we planned on sautéing.

Blackhawk was up top with a tall scotch and soda, and Indigo had some bouncy Michael Bublé' coming out of the Bose speakers. Her eyes were closed as she swayed rhythmically, occasionally taking a bite out of the margarita she had fixed for herself. She said no one else could make them as good as she could. She liked just the right amount of tequila and mix. Not too sweet. And she liked the good stuff. Elena, the tequila expert, asked Indigo to make one for her. Indigo fixed it and served it with a flair. Elena took a sip and nodded appreciatively. They both laughed.

I fixed a Plymouth on rocks with a small splash of bitters. It kept me company as I placed the small filets on the grill. I was met with a satisfying sizzle. I hovered. Good grilled meat requires hovering. Finally, all was ready. Elena had wrapped Ashley with a blue checkered apron I had. It was so large and Ashley so small she had to double wrap it. She made a thing out of calling Ashley her sous chef, and let her arrange the platters of food on the counter.

I took a plate of food up to Blackhawk. I offered to relieve him, but he waved me off. I think he was enjoying his peace and quiet.

"We may have to take it to them," he said.

"I've been thinking that," I said.

"We'll see tomorrow," he said.

"We'll see tomorrow," I repeated.

I went down, and they were waiting impatiently for me. Elena said her mama had taught her it was rude to start a meal before everyone was at the table.

Ashley's appetite impressed us. She ate like a wolf. Finally finished, we cleared the dishes. I washed and Indigo dried. She offered to do it all, but despite my rule of the cook doesn't clean, I made an exception.

When we finished, Elena gathered us on the floor of the lounge, surrounding the coffee table. We were going to play a card game that she and her cousins used to play. While Ashley was in her stateroom putting on a nightshirt, Elena explained that the name of the game was *shithead*. But, she said, in deference to small ears, we would call it *poopy head*.

Ashley thought this was hilarious. It was a simple game

with all the cards dealt out. The action is to discard. With the left of the dealer starting, and going clockwise, you discard a card higher in value than the last one discarded. If you don't have a higher card, you have to pick up all the discards. The object is to discard all of your cards, with the last one left being the poopy head. I was the first poopy head, and Ashley was gleefully delighted in singing along with the others, *Poopy head, poopy head, Jackson is a poopy head!*

Ashley thought it was the best game ever. We finally had to calls it quits after three long games. Ashley could have gone on all night. We put her to bed in the stateroom. The plan was that Indigo would sleep with her, Blackhawk and Elena would be in the master, and I would sleep up top on a chaise.

All the adults ended up with fresh drinks, sitting on top. The moon was up, and the stars were brilliant. The land mass surrounding us was a black wall. We talked softly for over an hour, then the girls decided to call it a night. They went down. Blackhawk and I sat silently together for another half hour, then he went down.

I went to sleep. There was a zero chance that those city bozos would find us in this cove, in the middle of the night. When I opened my eyes, the sky was just beginning to lighten. I wanted to make coffee, but I would have to go through the master stateroom, and I knew I would awaken Blackhawk. So I closed my eyes for another half hour. When a waft of coffee came to me, I knew someone was up. It was Blackhawk. He brought a mug up to me.

We sat, facing out over the bow. We watched the sky

brighten, changing colors, while we sipped the good coffee.

"How long do we wait?" Blackhawk said. "I'm not sure that those guys can even find us."

I nodded. "Give it a few hours."

"If they don't show, what do we do with the girl?"

"I've been thinking about that. I think we should talk to our old friend Father Correa."

"Good idea," he said.

Elena's head came over the edge, by the stairs. "I'm making pancakes," she said.

Blackhawk gave her a thumbs up and her head disappeared. Later, when she called up to us, we went down to eat.

It was after-noon when the snout of a rental Sea Ray sport boat showed around the corner three hundred yards away. I was up top, and I crabbed across the top and slid down the stairs. We all watched it from the interior darkness. It came to a halt and sat as they studied us. We had planned for this. We put Ashley in the master stateroom. Elena gave her the phone with earbuds and put something on it to keep her attention.

Indigo pumped a round into the Mossberg and wrapped it in a towel. She stuck the Beretta into the waistband of her bikini in the small of her back. She and Elena went up top. They studiously ignored the boat. They sat in the chaise lounges and began lathering with sunscreen. Just two girls taking in the sun. I went to the back where I would be unseen, and untied the stern line on Swoop. I retied the bow line, snugging it up against Tiger Lily one step away, where we could jump on and with one jerk of the line, be free.

I came back through the master and Ashley was propped up on the bed, engrossed in her show. I joined Blackhawk in the lounge, standing back out of the light. If the shit hit the fan, Elena was to bail and grab Ashley and get them both into the over-sized shower. Indigo would hold the high ground.

They were cautious. There were five of them. The Sea Ray was supposed to hold seven but these five filled it up. The guy at the wheel was sporting a billed captain's hat and binoculars. He had a white shirt and, although I couldn't see, I bet he had slacks, dark socks and brown shoes. He looked like the guy I had dumped into the lake.

Captain's hat was standing, giving us a good look. I was pretty sure they couldn't see anyone except the girls on top. He slowly moved the boat forward. He knew this was the Tiger Lily, but he had no idea who was on board. I pumped a shell into the other Mossberg, and Blackhawk slid a round into the chamber of his Sig Sauer.

Slowly the boat came closer. Elena and Indigo stood up and watched them. The Mossberg was lying on the chaise lounge, next to Indigo's hand. When the boat reached about twenty yards from us, Captain's hat yelled. "Hello there."

Elena and Indigo were silent.

"How are you ladies," he said with a big ol' smile.

"That's far enough," Indigo said.

Captain's hat turned and said something to the man behind him. The man stood, holding on to the boat. He put one foot up on the seat. It was obvious he was going to board.

"Who all is on board?" Captain's hat said.

"Who wants to know?" Elena said.

Captain's hat lifted a pistol off the console and showed it. "We do," he said. Now they were ten yards away, moving very slowly. Two of the other men stood.

Indigo reached down and brought up the Mossberg. She pointed it down and blew a big hole in the water in front of their bow. "Holy shit!" one of the men exclaimed. Indigo pumped a new round in and did it again.

Captain's hat twisted the wheel and jammed the throttle. The 200HP Evinrude roared and the boat spun, almost throwing two of the men out. Captain's hat had the throttle full open and they raced away.

Blackhawk and I went up top. Elena was laughing, hard. Indigo was in a stance, aiming the Beretta out over the water at the fleeing boat. She turned her head and looked at me. She winked.

"Well, now they know," Blackhawk said.

"Now they know."

31

They didn't come back. We sat inside playing board games until dusk. Finally, everyone but me went swimming. I sat up top, watching. When the sun was down, Elena, with Indigo's help, made what she called a Mexican bar. A counter filled with ground beef burros, tacos and enchiladas. Lawdy, lawdy it was good. Lawdy, lawdy it gave me gas.

Once again, we snugged all the blackout curtains, and the adults gathered up top when Ashley went to bed. Finally, one by one they trundled off to bed and I was left with the waning moon and a vast array of stars that would soon be hidden behind the bank of clouds that was coming in from the west. A breeze was up, bringing a front with it.

They knew where we were now, so I positioned my chair to face the entrance of the cove and stayed awake. I could hear the murmur of voices below. First Indigo and Elena, then Elena and Blackhawk, then finally silence.

I was dozing when I suddenly saw a twinkle of a light out at the entrance. It snapped me wide awake. The sky was completely covered, and it was dark as Hades. At first it had been just a twinkle, then it was gone. Then, there it was again, closer. This time it began to go on and off. Almost like Morris code. I picked up the Mossberg and went to the Captains chair in the cockpit. I waited.

It took twenty minutes for it to get close enough. I hit it with the hand-held 5-watt LED spotlight. It was so powerful I could light up the distant shore. It lit up the small skiff and the man in it. The man stood and raised his hands.

It was Eddie.

I took the light off of him and shone it back along the stern, so he could see to tie up. As he tied to us, I turned out the light. A moment later he came up the stairs. A moment after that Blackhawk followed. He carried three beers.

Eddie sat and nodded as Blackhawk handed him a beer. He took a long greedy drink.

"I was cleaning fish when I saw them boys come in. They all left, then about an hour later they showed up again and this time they took two boats. They filled one with camping stuff. I saw at least two automatic rifles. They took off together."

"They came back here?"

"My old Betsy couldn't keep up, but I came down here and did some fishing. They're just around the corner. They left two guys and the camping stuff. The other three went back to the harbor. I fished their shore line, minding my own business. They were setting up a camp at the top of the point. You come out of here, they'll call their friends. They'll catch you on open water."

"They hear you come in, just now?"

He shrugged. "Couldn't paddle this far."

"No way they'd put Eddie's boat with us," Blackhawk said.

"They saw him at the marina," I said. "They could've put binoculars on him."

"Different hat," Eddie said. "They were busy setting up their camp. They didn't even look at me. And it was getting dark. I went on down a ways and took a nap. Then I came here."

I sipped the beer and thought. They sat quietly. Finally, Blackhawk said, "We go neutralize them, then I have Nacho meet us and we take the girl to Father Correa."

I nodded. "Yeah," I said. "Except the we is Indigo and me. Elena is still skittish, and she won't want you leaving her alone."

He didn't say anything. Then he nodded.

I looked at Eddie. "You hang with us, and when Nacho picks us up, can you get the Lily back in her slip?"

"Sure."

"I'll go wake Indigo up," I said, standing.

"Indigo's already awake," she said standing on the stairs. "Let's get ready." She climbed back down.

32

I put on cargo shorts because of the extra pockets. I had another pair for Indigo, but we had to cinch her middle with a short piece of mooring line. We each filled the pockets with shells for the two Mossbergs. We each took a pistol, and I hooked on a fillet knife. We slipped on two of my black tee shirts.

The girls had shared a couple of bottles of wine, so I dug the cork from the wastebasket. I burned it and Elena used the blackened part to camouflage our face and arms. Swoop had two paddles in the long locker where water skis could be kept. She was a wide and stable boat. Stable enough so we could stand up and paddle. We climbed aboard, freed the line and pushed away.

We silently made our way around the Tiger Lily and staying close to the shore, we moved toward the mouth of the cove. A while back, Blackhawk, Elena, Detective First Grade Boyce and I had spent an extended time out on the lake. Several days had been in this cove. I was very familiar with it.

There was no reason to think the two goons on shore would be looking for us, but the cloud cover made us lucky. We were both carefully slipping the paddles in and out of the water silently. Every few minutes I took my bearings. It was really dark. After a long, slow trek, I suddenly saw a flicker of light at the top of the ridge. We stopped and looked at it.

"Campfire," Indigo said unnecessarily. Thirty yards ahead, I saw a dark lump on the shoreline. Their boat. I slipped my paddle in and pushed toward the shoreline. I carefully set the paddle down and stepped to the bow. I picked up the line and when the hull nudged the shore I stepped off. I held the boat while Indigo gathered the shotguns. She stepped off, set the shotguns down, and we both pulled the boat up, halfway onto the shore. I found a scrub sage and tied her off.

Indigo handed me a shotgun. We started up. She silently moved off about twenty yards. You never go up at an enemy in single file. It was dark and slow. Every step had the possibility of dislodging a rock. The ground was very rugged, and the creosote and cactus tugged at almost every step. We moved very slowly, carefully, setting our feet gently. And in the end, it didn't matter. Halfway up, we could hear their voices. They were arguing about the Phoenix Suns. One voice higher pitched and insistent, the other lower, gravely and slightly slurred. The noise allowed us to move faster. Whenever one of them was talking, we moved. We slowly crested the hill. They were sitting on either side of a fire in the kind of camp chairs that folded and were sold in a bag. I hated them. The chairs, not the guys. Oh, I might have hated them too, but right now I was pretty ambivalent. They were passing a bottle back and forth. This told me they were only here to make the call if the Tiger Lily pulled out of the cove.

I turned and looked for Indigo. She stepped out from behind a Palo Verde tree that had a branch broken and split off. The limb was lying on the ground, still attached to the trunk. The guys would be night blind, staring at the fire the way they were. Indigo looked over at me, waiting for me to take the lead.

I stepped into the firelight, the Mossberg casually pointed at a spot in between them.

"Which one of you guys do they call Machine Gun Kelly?" I said.

They froze. The one on my left had the bottle to his lips. He didn't move it. I could see the guy on the right thinking about making a move, then Indigo stepped out. Now there was no move to be had.

"Finish your drink," I said. The guy took the bottle from his lips. "Set it on the ground. Stand up and put your hands behind your head. Both of you." I waved the Mossberg. They stood and put their hands on their heads. Indigo moved behind them, took their hands, and in a not-so-gentle move, pulled their hands down behind their backs. She zip-tied them. One around the wrists, then another up through the middle. She pulled them snug and they both grunted when she did it. She frisked them. Each had a pistol. One a Smith and Wesson .32, the other a Colt Python. They didn't have the ARs. They did have phones, and the drinker had a pocket knife. Indigo pocketed the pistols.

To the side was a bundle that held a pop-up tent. They hadn't put it up. They were supposed to be watching all night. The tent was only if it rained. It hadn't rained all month. They had a cheap blue cooler. I looked in. It was full of beer. No food. They hadn't expected to be here long enough to get hungry.

Indigo fiddled with each of the phones, then handed them to me. "I sent the last five numbers they called to my phone," she said.

I nodded. I turned and threw each phone as far as I could. A moment later we heard two satisfying splashes. I threw the knife. It splashed. She picked up the whiskey bottle and poured it out. She started to throw it. I stopped her.

"Wait! I don't want broken glass in the lake."

Her eyebrows went up. "Phones and knives are okay. You think there's no glass in that lake?"

"Not that I put there," I said. "We'll carry it back."

One of the guys thought I was funny and snorted. Indigo smacked him in the mouth with the bottle. Blood spurted as he bent over with a strangled sound.

"Oh jeez, oh jeez," he moaned. He spit blood on the ground. He rose up. Blood was all over his chin and down the front of his shirt. I could see his front teeth were broken.

"You goddam bitch," he screamed at Indigo. Big mistake.

She punched him. It was a snap punch. A good one. The kind that comes straight from the shoulder with the weight of the body behind it. The kind where the fist twists slightly

168

just at impact. It caught the guy on his nose and he sat down with a thud. Broken nose, broken teeth. Wasn't his day.

She looked at the other guy, but he was shaking his head violently. He wasn't having any.

"Where's Lindy?" I said.

He looked at me blankly.

"The blonde girl. The girl's mother?"

He just looked at me. Indigo took a step toward him. He backed away, holding out the palm of his hand to ward her off. "Hold on, hold on."

"Where's Lindy?"

"I don't know. Newman has her stashed somewhere while we get the girl."

"Where?"

"I don't know." Indigo stepped again and he almost fell down. "No, really, I don't know. Newman went back to Vegas to be with his wife while we get the girl."

"What do you do when you get the girl?" Indigo asked.

"I don't know. Ted's in charge, I'm just supposed to call him if you guys move the boat."

"Ted the one that went into the water off my dock?"

The guy nodded.

"So, where do they have the girl's mother?"

"Shut up, Lenny!" the other guy mumbled through his broken mouth. Indigo swung backhanded, catching him on the back of the head with the bottle, and he went face first into the rock and cactus. He didn't move.

"Shit," Lenny said. "If they find out I'm talking to you guys, they'll kill me."

I pointed the Mossberg at him, "Your choice. Later or now."

His face was sick in the firelight. After a moment he said, "Newman keeps a house in Troon."

"That's where Lindy is?"

He shrugged. "Don't know her name, but that's the only place I know of."

I looked at Indigo. "Do you believe him?"

"Honest to God," the guy whined.

"She looked at me. "Yeah, I think I do. What do we do with them?"

I shook my head. "Nothing. We'll scuttle the boat. It'll take them half a day to walk out."

"Why don't we just kill them?" she said, raising the Mossberg.

The guy's eyes grew very wide. "Oh, no no no," he moaned.

She grinned and leaned toward him, "I'm just joshing ya." The guy was about to wet himself. Tough guy with little girls.

"Let's get back," I said. I turned, and we started back down the slope. This time we didn't care about noise. She stood beside Swoop as I untied their boat. I pushed it out a little, so it was floating. I untied Swoop's bow line and we pushed it out. We stepped on board and this time I fired the motor. I put her in gear and angled her toward the other boat.

When we reached her I said, "Grab the line."

She leaned off the bow and got the other boat's line in her hand. "Hold on," I said. I gently moved the throttle and we slid out away from the shore. When we were far enough, I put us in neutral. I stood and picked up the Mossberg. I came around and climbed up on the bench seat. I leaned down and pointed the tip of the Mossberg's barrel about two inches off the bottom. I blew a hole in it. The noise was deafening, and it rolled across the lake.

My ears were ringing. Indigo stuck a finger in hers and wiggled it. "Shit, Jackson! You won't throw a bottle into the lake, but you'll dump a whole fucking boat."

33

The cloud cover had broken slightly, so there was a little more visibility when we nudged up to the Tiger Lily. Elena, Blackhawk and Eddie were waiting. Blackhawk was up top, Elena on the bow, and Eddie at the stern waiting to tie us off. He had given his skiff more line and had shoved it out of the way. Indigo clambered up the stern and handed Swoop's bow line to Eddie. He tied it off. I lifted the motor until it locked into place. She would trail behind now.

As I came on board, Elena came through the sliding doors to the stern. It was crowded, so Indigo slipped out of the oversized cargo shorts and went up the stairs.

"I heard a shot," Elena said.

I could hear Indigo laugh. "Jackson killed a boat," she said. "Limited out."

Elena was looking at me. It wasn't funny.

"Eddie was right. There were two of them. We neutralized them. It will be several hours before they find anyone to help them."

"They're alive?" she said.

"Jackson wouldn't let me kill them," Indigo said from above.

"That isn't funny," Elena said.

To change the subject, I looked up at Blackhawk. He was outlined against the dark sky. "Did you get a hold of Nacho?"

"Yeah. Took ten minutes to get him awake enough to make sense. I don't know what the hell has gotten into him lately. Like he's just exhausted all the time."

Indigo punched him in the shoulder.

Blackhawk laughed, rubbing his arm, "He's bringing the van to the Castle Creek ramp. We'll meet him there."

I looked at Eddie. "Think you can get the Lily and both boats back okay?"

"Cake," he said. "I'll just tie them off on each side, so they don't bump. I'll tie Lily off at the end of the dock and put mine away, then put the Grumman away, then the Lily."

"How's the girl?" I said to Elena.

"Sound asleep," she said.

"Great," I said. I looked up at Blackhawk. "Let's go."

Eddie took his boat, and Indigo drove Swoop. It took us an hour to work our way across the water. As we passed the mouth of the cove, someone above was shouting some very dirty words at us. The sound was mushed up, like maybe the guy had some kind of trouble with his mouth.

I knew the lake very well and Eddie knew it better. We had no problem crossing in the dark. Indigo followed Eddie. When we finally reached the ramp, the eastern sky was just beginning to lighten. The ramp already had two early morning fishermen launching their boats. We had beat Nacho. We all moored to the side of the ramp and waited. Elena made coffee.

When the sun was full up, Ashley was awake and eating Fruit Loops. The ramp had filled before Nacho appeared. We were all in the galley. Elena had scrambled eggs and fried bacon with Indigo toasting bagels when Blackhawk came down from the sun deck.

"Nacho's here," he said.

I was surprised at the grin that came onto Indigo's face. Elena looked at me, shaking her head, smiling. Indigo set the cream cheese aside and went out on the bow. She jumped ashore and started up the hill. Nacho stood at the top waiting. When she reached him, Indigo gave a whoop and jumped on him, her arms around his neck, and her legs around his waist. He was too far away, but I swore his dark face was beet red.

Blackhawk came into the galley and was looking out the front window.

"Who'd a thunk it," he said.

Ashly looked up from her cereal bowl. "She really likes that guy," she said with a grin.

Elena took Blackhawk around the neck and kissed him. "Don't expect it to last," she said.

"Why do you say that?"

She smiled up into his face. "Those are two wild butterflies that just happened to land on the same flower."

"Butterflies?" I said.

I watched them a second, then I looked at Blackhawk.

"We can leave most of this stuff on the boat. Let's just take what we may need."

"Like the shotguns," he said.

"Like the shotguns."

We packed what we wanted off the boat. Nacho drove down so we wouldn't have to carry it up. I helped Eddie tie off the two skiffs, one to each corner of Tiger Lily's stern. He fired her up and Blackhawk and I pushed them out. Eddie stayed in reverse until he had enough room for a wide turn.

I held Ashley's hand. Nacho and Indigo stood waiting.

"Where to?" Nacho said. Ashley was watching him with cautious eyes. Nacho intimidated most people. He was tall, wide and muscled. He usually wore a black tee with some hard rock motif. His face was broad and craggy, like he'd been punched too many times. Ashley moved around behind me.

"This is my friend, Nacho," I said.

"He's scary," she said.

Elena and Indigo laughed. Nacho knelt down to get to her eye level.

"I'm not scary," he said. "I'm just a big old puddy cat. Can you make faces?" He crossed his eyes, stuck a finger in each side of his mouth and pulled as he stuck his tongue out.

Ashley's eyes grew wider. "My mom says you shouldn't do that because your eyes may stick that way."

Nacho pulled his fingers from his mouth, but left his eyes crossed. He stood up and smacked himself in his head. "Oh, no. My eyes are stuck." He knelt down again. "Here, quick. Hit me on the head."

Ashley hesitated, then reached over and lightly tapped him on the head. His eyes went to normal.

"Oh, thank you very much," he grinned. "My eyes are normal now."

Ashley grinned. "You're just trickin'."

"He's a trickster, all right," Indigo said.

"Let's head downtown," Blackhawk said.

As we piled in, Nacho said, "What's the plan?"

"We're going to see if Father Correa can help us," I said.

"Good idea," Nacho said.

34

"Bad idea," Father Correa said.

Blackhawk and I had left Ashley in the van with Indigo and Nacho. Elena was with us.

"We're only talking a couple of days," I said.

We were in Father Correa's tight office, which had not changed one paper clip from the day I first met him.

He smiled at me. He always smiled. I don't know what unbearable disaster would have to occur for him to not smile.

"Jackson, you know you hold a very special place in my heart. God and I will be forever grateful for the blessings you and Mr. Blackhawk here, have bestowed on Safehouse. But first of all, we're full. I don't have a bed in the place, and…"

"What blessings?" Elena said.

"I beg your pardon?" Father Correa said.

She was looking at Blackhawk. "What blessings? You have been here before?"

Blackhawk looked at her. Father Correa glanced at me.

I spoke quickly. "You know Father Correa helps young

women in trouble. Usually, young mothers with no place to go," I said. "He helped me with a couple of young women I knew that needed help."

Blackhawk was looking at me, his face impassive.

"So, in return," I continued, "Blackhawk helped me get him a new washing machine and some other appliances. Just stuff like that."

Elena reached over and patted Blackhawk on the arm. "That's sweet, honey."

"So just a couple of days," I said to Father Correa.

Now Father Correa reached over and patted me on the hand. "She's too young. She's alone, and I don't have a bed." He looked at Elena. "I have young women here, and many of them have children with them, but at the same time, many of them are very troubled. Many of them are addicts, and most are not, how should I say this, um, not of the higher end of our society, either economically, or educationally. In other words, your little girl would be alone and exposed to things that a little girl shouldn't be exposed to."

"She's already exposed to Jackson," Elena said.

Father Correa smiled. Blackhawk smiled. I didn't know whether to smile or not.

"Any suggestions?" I said.

He shook his head. You could tell he wasn't happy he couldn't help us.

"From what you've told me I think the best course of action is to turn her over to the authorities."

"Child Protective Services?"

He nodded.

"Would you turn a child over to them?"

He shrugged. "Depending on the circumstance."

"How about this circumstance?"

He looked at me for a long time. Finally, he said, "Only if you can't keep her safe."

35

We were back in the apartment above the El Patron. At least they had a television. Elena found the Disney channel and settled Ashley in their bedroom to watching Doc McStuffins. Nacho and Indigo were downstairs prepping the bar for the evening. At least that's what they said they were going to do. Elena had showered and was now in the midst of the laborious job of applying the perfect makeup. Despite the lack of sleep last night, she had decided to perform tonight. She didn't want to let the band down. They relied on the income.

Blackhawk was on the expensive burgundy leather Victorian chair Elena had selected. I was on the couch rubbing my stub.

There was a knock on the door. Blackhawk said, "Come on in."

Jimmy stepped in. "You wanted to see me, boss?"

Blackhawk waved him in. He looked at me. "I thought Jimmy could help us find which place in Troon belongs to Newman."

"Good idea."

"Yes, it is." He stood, "Let's go into the office."

I attached my foot and followed him out the door. Jimmy followed me. We stepped out into the hallway and turned right to Blackhawk's office. Jimmy and I followed Blackhawk into the office. Blackhawk waved Jimmy to sit at the desk. "You guys want something to drink?" he asked.

Jimmy declined.

"No thanks," I said. "What I'd like is about five hours of sleep."

"What are we looking for?" Jimmy said, tapping the keyboard of the desktop to bring it alive.

"Guy named Donald Newman. Vegas big shot. Mob connected developer. Guy owns a property in Troon. What I'm figuring is the property is probably owned by a corporation. So we need to look for businesses he's affiliated with, then see if the county assessor site has a match on properties in that area."

"Got it," Jimmy said. "Middle initial?"

I shrugged. "Don't know. But he was the developer of the golf community *Quail Run* in Vegas. Maybe you can track him down from there."

Jimmy nodded. "It may take a while."

"Good, I'll get some sleep." I stretched out on the couch, turned my back to the room and went to sleep. We had been taught to sleep when you need it. I could tune everything out and be asleep in seconds. I'd also learned how to awaken to an internal clock. I didn't set it, expecting them to wake me when they found something.

When I opened my eyes, Blackhawk's office was dark. And empty. Except for me. I went into the small bathroom that was off to the side and washed my face and drank out of the faucet. I took out my phone to look at the time. I'd slept for three hours. I went to his bar and got a bottle of water. I went to the far wall and pulled the curtains to look out the two-way mirror. It over-looked the bar area. The bar was empty except for Blackhawk and Jimmy working inside the rectangled bar. I went downstairs.

I went to my usual stool, by the corner. Jimmy brought a Dos Equis and sat it in front of me. I sipped on it and watched Blackhawk. Every move was like poetry. Finally, he came over and looked at me.

"So you gonna tell me if you found something?" I said.

"You needed your beauty sleep."

"So do you."

"I'll get mine."

"What did you find?"

"I'll have Jimmy tell you." He signaled Jimmy.

Jimmy came over. "The guy is involved in a number of companies. C corps, S corps, a lot of LLCs. One of them is Avalon Inc. Avalon Inc. is a land holding company. One of the pieces of land it owns is a horse property on the way to Rio Verde."

"Down the road from Troon," Blackhawk said. "You know where Dynamite Road is?"

I nodded.

Jimmy continued. "Go east far enough on Dynamite Road and you'll run smack into Rio Verde. It's a golf community. I mean just that. Golf. Nothing else. Lucky to have a Circle K. Well, this Avalon property is on the way out Dynamite on the way to Rio Verde."

"So, you think this is where Lindy is?"

Blackhawk said, "Neighbors are far apart. The horse properties run up to ten, twelve acres apiece. People out there like their privacy. And many of them have guest houses."

"How do you know this stuff?"

"Tomas Marino, the casino manager, lives out there. He tries to impress me with how much money he has. Likes to brag. Has the big horse property, but no horses. Doesn't like animals."

"All hat, no cattle."

"Exactly. So, what do you want to do about it."

"Go visit, I guess. We need to find out if Lindy is there."

"How we going to do that?"

"Good question. Can't just walk up and ring the doorbell. She won't be the one answering."

He reached over and took my empty. "I need sleep," he said. "Elena needs sleep. Lord knows Indigo will need sleep."

I laughed. "Not to mention Nacho."

He smiled. "He doesn't know what hit him. Anyway, Ashley is good, here. Whatever we do can wait till tomorrow. We'll figure it out tomorrow."

Jimmy said, "You guys want anything else?"

We both shook our heads.

He started to move away, then turned back. "Oh, I think I forgot to tell you."

We both looked at him.

"When I was looking through all the companies that that Newman guy was hooked up with, I saw one that sounded familiar."

"Which one?"

"Sussex Financial. Wasn't that what that other dude was hooked up with?"

We looked at each other.

"Luis," we said simultaneously.

36

I was worried about the Tiger Lily, and I was still tired, and I didn't like the idea of a couple of punks keeping me away from my own place. I figured Newman might still have someone watching the marina, but I didn't care. If I couldn't handle that, I should probably hang it up. I took a Lyft car to the marina. I had him pull up close enough to the parking area for me to look it over really good.

They had a new kid running the shuttle. I slipped on a ball cap, sunglasses and tipped the driver. I got out and waved at the shuttle driver. He slid up next to me and I climbed aboard. As we went down the hill, I checked every person and every boat. Nothing looked amiss.

I tipped the shuttle driver and went inside the marina store. Maureen was behind the counter, stocking power drinks. Those things never made sense to me. You want a caffeine jolt, drink more coffee. She looked up.

"Hey, Jackson," she said.

"Good day to you," I said. "You seen any strangers lurking about?"

"They are all strangers," she said. "But no, no lurkers."

"Eddie working?"

"He's in the bar."

"Thanks."

He indeed was in the bar. He was the only one. He was wiping down the liquor bottles. He was the only one that ever did it.

"You have any trouble?"

He shook his head. "You want a beer?"

I shook my head. "I just want a few hours sleep."

"Don't know what I expected, when I brought the boats in, but none of those guys were here. Maybe you've scared them off."

"I doubt it. Not as long as I have the little girl."

"Where is she?"

"Blackhawk. Come on down later, we'll have a beer."

"Get some rest," he said, putting the Seagram's bottle back in place.

I turned away.

"By the way," he said. "You might check your carburetor. Seemed a little rasty. Probably just needs cleaning."

I nodded and went out the back way. I went down the dock and walked by the Thirteen Episodes. The curtains were back but it was dark inside. Maybe Pete had his Western done.

I stepped aboard the Tiger Lily and automatically checked my alarms. Of course, they were off. Eddie didn't know about them. No one did except Blackhawk. Blackhawk knew because he knew I would have something like them in place, and he had searched them out. I activated them and went inside.

It looked like what it would look like. A lot of people had been aboard. I straightened things up, made a sandwich. Drank a cold glass of milk, pulled off the foot and lay on the king-sized bed.

I awoke to the Lily thudding up against her bumpers. I could hear the wind was up. I felt rested. That felt good. I rolled off the bed and hopped to the back curtains. I pulled them aside and slid the double doors open. The clouds were dark and rolling, and the breeze had dropped a good twenty degrees. The lake had a cake topping of white-caps.

I hopped to the closet and got my swim foot. I slipped into my faded USMC swim trunks. The water was warmer than the air. I started swimming laps to the buoy and back. I didn't count.

It began to rain. Then the lightning cracked on the far side just as I reached the buoy. I held on. I bobbed in the water, watching. I watched a wall of rain slide across the lake. When it hit me, it came down in sheets. Thunder rolled across the water with an almost physical presence. I know it was dumb and foolish to be out on the water with the lightening cracking all around, but it was exhilarating. I found myself grinning like a fool. If I was going to go, this was a whole lot better than some hospital bed.

After a few minutes, the rain began to lessen, but the wind was still blowing. Something caught my attention back in the marina. I swiveled my head to see Eddie and his skiff come put-putting out. Eddie had a yellow slicker and hat. He looked like a north shore lobster man. I watched as he came closer. He struggled with the wind keeping the boat on course. His course was to me.

As he got close, he yelled above the wind. "You okay? You need help?"

I grinned at him and gave him a thumb's up.

He shook his head. "You damn fool," he shouted. "You could get killed out here."

He maneuvered the skiff next to me, and I pulled myself up and in. He was looking at me like I was crazy. Maybe I was.

"Sorry, I was just swimming."

He shook his head with disgust and started back to the Tiger Lily. When he bumped the stern, I stepped aboard and snugged the bow line off. He clambered aboard. It was awkward with the heavy rubber slicker. I went in, changed feet, and opened the lounge drapes as Eddie stepped out of the slicker and into the back stateroom.

I pulled a bottle of Wild Turkey and two glasses. "Make it three," Eddie said, coming into the galley. He nodded toward the bow. I turned to look, and Pete was stepping onboard.

He came in, shaking the rain off, like a wet dog.

"What the hell were you doing out there?" He surprised me. He wasn't looking at me, he was talking to Eddie.

I had to laugh.

"I thought I was saving this damn fool," Eddie said.

Pete looked puzzled.

"I was swimming," I said. "Eddie thought I was in trouble."

"It was goddam lightning," Eddie said. "You don't screw around with lightning."

"I appreciate a good friend thinking of me," I said.

"Well, give your good friend a drink, goddammit."

"Make it three," Pete said. So I poured three.

"I'm glad you're here," I said. "I've got a problem, and I need a solution."

"The first part of solving a problem is realizing you have a problem."

"Well, thank you, Tony fucking Robbins," Eddie said, knocking his drink back.

"I wish you wouldn't cuss in front of the children," Pete said.

Eddie's eyebrows went up. He looked behind him. "That little girl isn't here, is she?"

"I was talking about Jackson," Pete said. "Tell us what the problem is."

So I did.

37

Pete had followed me back downtown to the El Patron. The band was practicing for the evening gig. We were at the bar with Blackhawk, Nacho and Indigo. Jimmy was behind the bar, serving. He served us each a beer. Except Blackhawk. He had club soda and tonic.

"As usual, Pete had a good idea."

"Idea for what?" Nacho said.

"We pretty well nailed down where we think Ashley's mother is. Where she's being held. It's in a horse property out Dynamite Road, between Scottsdale and Rio Verde. But the trick is to figure out if she is really there, without tipping those guys off."

"Surveillance?" Indigo said.

"The problem there is how long do we have to do that? They could keep her in there for a month. Keep her inside, out of sight."

"So what did you come up with?" Blackhawk said, looking at Pete.

"Send in a package she has to sign for."

"They could just ignore it," Indigo said.

"Yeah, we thought of that," I said. "So we send a package from Newman with his Vegas address as the return address. She has to come to the door to sign for it. If she's not there, they'll tell us."

"Might work," Nacho said.

"Then what?" Indigo said. "We find out she's there, then what? Just bust the door down and go in and get her? She could get hurt."

"I've been thinking about that," I said.

"And?" Blackhawk said.

"And, we need to communicate with her. We want her beside a door, or window of our choosing, at a certain time. Middle of the night, probably. We crack the window, or the door and take her out before they can react."

"How do we communicate?" Blackhawk said.

"This is the brilliant part," Pete said. He looked at me. "Jackson's idea. Tell them."

"Jesus, that'll go to his head," Blackhawk said.

I ignored him. "We can figure her guards will open the package and look it over. So what it will be is a very feminine bottle of perfume or lotion. It will have a cap on it."

Indigo laughed. "Perfume. The first thing a woman does is spray her wrist for a smell. There's not a guy alive that would do that."

"We shrink wrap it with the label on the outside, so they can see exactly what it is and who's sending it. The message….."

"Is in the cap," Indigo said.

We were all smiling.

Blackhawk sent Nacho to find a cheap magnetic sign that turned the band van into a delivery van. Pete volunteered to be the delivery boy. We bought a uniform, down to the cap, brown shorts, black socks and black shoes. We fixed up a clip-board with the right paper work. Indigo and I went perfume shopping. I thought we should go to Scottsdale Fashion Square, maybe to Nordstrom's or something upscale like that. She took me to Walmart.

"We need a bottle with a big lid," she explained. I'm not sure how Walmart went with big lids, but I went along. Sure enough, we found what we needed. Back at the nightclub I fashioned the note. I cut a strip of paper that was less wide than the lid. I wrote, *"Mark a window with soap that you can be beside, and ready to go, at 2AM,- Jackson"*. I wound it inside the lid. Then we shrink-wrapped the bottle and attached the label.

We waited till late afternoon. We had looked at the property with satellite imaging from Google Earth. It was just past 141st Street, off Dynamite Road by almost a hundred yards. It was large with a meandering dirt drive that ended up in front. It was surrounded by a wall that went around the entire property. In the back there was a large grass expanse inside the wall. Behind the grass was the area with corrals, and a barn. Immediately behind the main house was a large pool, shaped to be more lagoon like than a swimming pool rectangle. There was a neighbor quite a way back from the south wall, but other than that, it was pretty isolated.

Blackhawk and I went first. 141st Street was dirt. I drove a hundred yards up it and pulled off. Taking the Nikon ten-power binoculars, we found a spot where we were hidden, but had a clear view of the front door. I looked at my watch. We had fifteen minutes. Pete was due at 6 pm. If we got lucky they would be eating or getting ready to eat. I was figuring none of these guys could boil water, so they would probably have Lindy do the cooking. I knew she could make mac and cheese because Ashley told me so.

Pete was on time. He brought a cloud of dust with him. He pulled up to the area in front of the house. I call it area, because it was just a wide patch of dirt. He was smart enough to park as far back as he could, to lessen the scrutiny of the van from the front door.

I adjusted the binoculars as he carried the package up to the front door. We had placed the address and return address label on the clear shrink wrap. There was no question as to who it was from. This was key. I watched as he rang the doorbell. He waited. He rang again.

"What if they don't answer?" Blackhawk said.

"Then we go to plan B."

"What's plan B?

"I don't know," I said as the door opened. I watched the pantomime as Pete explained he needed Lindy's signature. The guy reached for the package. Pete stepped back. He held out the clipboard, explaining he needed her signature. We had rehearsed this part, figuring they'd give him a hard time. I could see him shaking his head. He couldn't relinquish the package without her signature.

The goon looked disgusted, but he disappeared inside. Pete was good. He didn't look across the desert to where he knew we would be. It was a long moment. I began to worry. Then the door opened, and Lindy stepped out. Bingo!

She signed for the package. Pete said something to her and turned and went back to the truck. This was rehearsed also. He was to say, his wife thought that stuff was the best smelling stuff in the world. We wanted her to be sure to open it. She stepped inside and closed the door. Pete fired the truck up and backed out the drive, then turned back toward Scottsdale.

At one forty-five in the morning, Blackhawk and I were lucky. Lindy had followed instructions and had marked a window on the west side of the house. She had been liberal with the soap and the X was large and prominent. The room behind the window was dark. The drapes were drawn. Now I was hoping Lindy was just on the other side of the window. We didn't want to have to go in and get her. We were dressed alike, in dark clothes, dark watch caps and rubber-soled shoes. We were armed, and I carried a ten-pound hammer. I felt like Thor, God of Thunder. Aaargh.

Indigo was pissed we hadn't included her. I carefully explained that the Mustang had the most muscle of any of our vehicles. If we had to run, I wanted to run fast. And the Mustang was barely big enough for three. I carefully explained, it wasn't big enough for four. She didn't care, she was still pissed.

Waiting for five minutes to pass can be excruciating. Finally, the illuminated hands on my watch showed two o'clock, straight up. Blackhawk threw the master breaker switch and in three massive swings I took the window out. Despite the breaker, an alarm started screeching. I reached inside, grabbed a handful of drape and pulled it loose. I yanked it through the window, leaving enough to cover the broken glass on the sill.

"Lindy?" I said.

"I'm here," her voice came from the dark inside.

"Let's go," I said, holding a hand out, into the dark room. She took my hand and clambered out the window. I could hear shouting inside the house. Blackhawk was back with us, and we turned and ran toward the Mustang. Because of the scrub brush and cactus, we had planned the route ahead. It wasn't a straight line. Even with the planning, it was tough. Plants grabbing at our legs in the dark. Lindy stumbled and went to one knee. We both pulled her up and got her going again. We went over the wall and reached the Mustang just as the emergency floodlights lit up. Luckily, they illuminated the property inside the wall, not outside.

Blackhawk shoved Lindy into the back seat.

"Stay down on the floor board," he said as he climbed in.

I fired her up. I blew dirt and dust behind me, as I roared toward the street. I fish-tailed onto Dynamite Road, and the tires grabbed purchase with a long ear-splitting squeal. Blackhawk was turned in the seat.

"You're going the wrong way," he said.

"I'm going to Rio Verde. If they didn't see us they'll think I went to Scottsdale."

"Good idea," he said. "Except they saw you, and here they come."

Sure enough, I watched the lights pop out behind me. I goosed it. There are no streetlights out here, and it was like I was driving in a tunnel. I could feel Lindy sit up behind me.

"Where's Ashley?" she said.

"She's safe."

She was quiet a moment, then, "Who the hell are you guys?"

38

"Lindy, this is Blackhawk. Blackhawk, Lindy."

"Pleased to meet you," Blackhawk said.

"Blackhawk? What kind of name is Blackhawk? You an Indian or something?"

"Oh, he's something," I said.

"Are you sure Ashley's okay?"

"You explain kemo sabe, me drive," I said to Blackhawk.

I was really concentrating on the ribbon of road. I knew up ahead was a sharp right-hand turn and I wanted to make sure we made it.

"Ashley is with our people," Blackhawk said above the roar of the engine. "She is very safe." He glanced over at me. "When you didn't come back to Jackson's boat, he enlisted our help in taking care of Ashley. She is a very bright little girl," he said.

"Who's your help?"

"Friends of Jackson. Very competent friends. Your friend, Mr. Newman, sent his people to collect Ashley, and Jackson objected, not sure if that was your wishes."

"He objected?"

"Very strongly."

"He isn't my friend. Newman, I mean. I was working for him when I got pregnant. He didn't want anything to do with me or the baby after that. Then things changed, and he did."

"No doubt Newman is the father?"

"Oh yes, there is doubt."

"Did you do a DNA test?"

She shook her head, but I didn't see it. "Nope. Didn't want to."

"Because you might find out he is the father?"

She was silent for a long moment, then she evidently had turned to look out the back window. "Those guys are getting closer," she said.

I glanced in the rear view and she was right. Up ahead the high beams hit the yellow sign with the black arrow, and then we were sliding into the curve. As the rear tires caught traction again, I hit the accelerator. Lindy was bouncing around in the back.

"Buckle up," Blackhawk said to Lindy.

Rio Verde is a sleepy little golf course burg. Far enough away to avoid the hustle and bustle. People moved here to play golf. They arose in the morning, drank their orange juice and whatever healthy buzzard puke green stuff they had concocted in their blenders, then went to make their tee times. After the game they played cards in the clubhouse, sometimes dined there, then went to the latest cocktail party. Next morning, they started all over again.

The main drag is on the east side and goes the entire length of the town, which is to say a couple of miles. There are stoplights, but not at this time of the night. I blew through them, reaching up to eighty miles per hour. Off toward the darkness on the east, the Verde River trickles along. On the south side of town, the road does another right hand and the winding highway takes you to Fountain Hills. I went through the entire town of Rio Verde in about thirty seconds.

The road to Fountain Hills is twisty and I put the Mustang through her paces. This is why you have a vehicle like the Mustang. This is where it's fun. The headlights behind me had disappeared.

Finally, from the dark of the back seat, Lindy said, "I don't get it. Why?"

"Why what?" Blackhawk said.

"Why didn't you just give Ashley to Newman?" she said to me.

"Wasn't mine to give," I said.

"What's that mean?"

Blackhawk hitched around. "You asked Jackson to watch her while you were gone. You had not given permission to hand her to anyone," he said. "Jackson plays to his own set of rules. Sometimes, I don't even get it. But you can count on the fact that he will never waver from his set of rules. You hadn't given him permission to give her to anyone."

"So you would keep her forever?"

"Not forever," I said. "But I would make sure she would be safe and happy. How much do you know about his business dealings?" I said, to change the subject.

"Not much," she said. "Why?"

"You ever hear of a company named Sussex Financial?"

She was silent, thinking. "No, doesn't ring a bell. Newman was involved with a lot of companies. I was the real estate girl, so if they weren't developers, I probably wouldn't know them."

"Newman ever involved with sex trafficking that you knew of?"

"No, why do you ask that?"

"We did some research on Newman. That's how we found you. One of the companies he's involved with owns that house you were in."

"I was wondering about that."

"We found he was on the board of another company, Sussex Financial. Another guy we knew was involved with Sussex Financial. That guy was heavy into the sex trade."

"Ugh," she said. We rode in silence for a long time.

Then she said, "I told you about those parties I would go to with him?"

"Yeah."

"There was a creep that came to those. Don treated him like a big shot. He always brought a half-dozen young girls with him and he always had a half dozen tough looking guys with him."

"Tough like Don's guys?"

"Oh no, tougher than that. Mostly Hispanics, gang looking. Tattoos, like that."

"What was the guy's name?"

She thought a minute. "I don't remember."

The lights of Fountain Hills came into sight.

She was silent for a long time. Finally, she said, "You guys don't know Don Newman. He can be ruthless. He could just have you killed. He wouldn't blink an eye."

"You have never met anyone harder to kill," Blackhawk said.

39

I pulled into a resort in Scottsdale that had a parking garage. It was early in the morning and Lindy had dozed off in the back seat. Every time I had glanced at Blackhawk, he was wide awake. Talk about a set of personal rules.

I dropped Blackhawk and Lindy at the front and found a place to park in the garage. I had picked the place at random. I was confident we wouldn't be found. If the sleepy desk clerk found it odd we had no luggage, she didn't show it. Our room was on the second floor. We raided the vending machine in the hallway. We had two king beds. Blackhawk and I stretched out on one, Lindy on the other. With the lights out, it was pitch black. We were asleep in seconds.

When I opened my eyes, light was struggling to come in around the black-out curtains. I looked at my watch. It was 8:30. Blackhawk and I sat up at the same time. Lindy was still down. She was on her side, her blonde hair lying across her face.

"She needs to see Ashley," I said.

"We can get something to eat and a shower at my place," Blackhawk said.

I slipped my shoes on, then reached over and gently shook Lindy's shoulder. She muttered something. I shook her again.

"Time to go, honey," I said.

She stretched out and opened her eyes. "Ashley?" she said.

"Time to wake up. We are going to see Ashley."

Without a word, she sat up, then stood, then went into the bathroom. In a moment she came back out, Her face damp. Blackhawk took his turn, then I did mine. They were sitting on the beds waiting when I came out. We went down and I paid for the room in cash. This time the clerk gave us the eye. Like, what did those two perverts do to that poor little girl?

After some maneuvers to insure we weren't followed, and thirty minutes later I was parking behind the El Patron.

We went in through the back storeroom. We went across the bar and up the steps. The apartment was quiet. After a night of performing, Elena usually slept until eleven. Indigo heard us and came out of the bedroom she shared with Ashley. I introduced her.

"You're the Mama?" she said. She nodded toward the closed door. "She's still sleeping. She had trouble getting to sleep last night. You can go in and wake her. She's your baby."

"I have to see her," Lindy said softly.

Indigo quietly opened the door and Lindy went in. Ashley was lying face down in a tangle of covers. Lindy moved to the bed and sat beside her. She began to stroke her hair. After a while, Ashley stirred. It took her a few moments to open her eyes. When she did, they got wide.

"Mama!"

"Hey baby, I'm back."

Ashley threw her arms around Lindy's neck and Lindy began to cry. Indigo quietly shut the door.

We went into the living room. "I'm famished," I said.

Indigo looked at me. "I ain't your little woman. Do your own cooking."

"Hey, calm down, turbo. I'm not asking you to cook. You still pissed about last night?"

She shrugged her shoulders. "I just wanted to go."

"There wasn't room," Blackhawk said. He yawned. "I'm going to go in and snuggle with my little woman. Help yourself to whatever you find."

"You hungry?" I said to Indigo.

"Does the pope shit in the woods?"

40

Ashley took great delight in telling her mother about our houseboat trip and swimming in our *diapers,* and especially about me being the *poopy head.* I felt like I was beginning to smell, so I decided to make the trek out to the boat.

Again, there were no lurkers. I expected them this time, thinking they might decide we would bring Lindy back here after her escape. But nope. No lurkers. I showered, took a nap, took a swim, made a giant sandwich and headed back to the El Patron. I needed to talk to Lindy. I needed more information on Don Newman. And I wanted to know about the guy that brought the girls to Newman's parties.

It was about six when I pulled into the parking lot. The bar was open, with a sizable number of downtown business types enjoying their happy hour. I waved at Jimmy and went upstairs. I knocked at the apartment door.

Ashley opened the door, with Lindy trying to get to it first.

"Ashley, honey. Mommy doesn't want you to open the doors," Lindy said, looking flustered.

"Hey kiddo," I said. "Can I come in?"

"Hey, Jackson. You want to play checkers?"

Lindy smiled at me. "Honey, Jackson just got here. Let him relax a minute."

She pulled Ashley back, so I could enter. There was a tantalizing odor coming from the kitchen. Blackhawk came into the room. "You want a drink?"

"Sure," I said. Blackhawk went to the bar and started fixing drinks without asking what I wanted. He already knew.

Elena looked around the corner from the kitchen, "Oh, it's you," she said. "As usual, right on time for supper."

"It's a gift," I said, taking my drink from Blackhawk.

"You want to play checkers?" Ashley said.

"I need to talk to your mamma, honey. Maybe later."

"Come on Hon," Lindy said. "Let's get something on TV for you." She led the girl into the bedroom.

Blackhawk took his drink and sat on the Victorian chair. In a minute Lindy came back in.

"You want a drink?" Blackhawk said.

She shook her head. She came over and sat beside me. I took a small bite of the drink. She was looking at me.

"I don't really know who you are," she said. She looked at Blackhawk. "I don't know who any of you are." She looked back to me. "I was talking to that other woman."

"Indigo," I said.

"Yes. She is very unusual. I mean, look at her name. She seems very, uh, tough. She frightens me a little bit."

"She's on your side."

"And I'm glad of it, but I started asking her questions, and she told me things that are too fantastical to be true. She talks like you two are supermen. She says you were all on the same team. But she really wouldn't tell me what kind of team. She told me you worked for the government, and you had special skills. She also told me you didn't lose your foot in an industrial accident. It was blown off by one of those IED bomb things while you were on some kind of mission."

"You are safe with us," Blackhawk said.

"I know that," she said. "I don't know why I know that, but I know that. I know you all took care of Ashley." She looked at me. "I was thinking about what you asked me. About that guy that brought girls to Don's parties. I think Don called him Bill."

I looked at Blackhawk. "So we look for someone associated with Sussex named Bill." I looked back to Lindy. "How did Newman get his hands on you?" I said. "After you left us."

She put her face in her hands. She shook her head. She looked up at me. Her eyes were wet. "I was a fool. When I went off to do that shopping, I decided that Don would be reasonable. So I called him. He was very receptive. We talked in a way we hadn't talked before. He just wanted to help Ashley. He promised to take care of us. Somehow, he figured out where I was, so while I was on the phone with him, his men came and grabbed me. Literally picked me up and threw me into the backseat of a car." She rubbed her face. "They took the money you gave me, so I guess I owe you."

I shrugged. "Tell me about some things I've been

wondering. Like, how do you know he's Ashley's father. You said you didn't have a DNA test done."

She shook her head. "He doesn't care about her, not really. I don't know why he's doing this." She sat staring at the rug for a long time. It's a nice rug, but probably not worth that kind of scrutiny. She looked up and took a deep breath, "And it's quite probable he's not the father. I was his party girl, but I was mostly his arm candy. We didn't have relations but maybe twice. And I was on birth control."

"Did you have relations with other men?" Blackhawk said.

She nodded. "I was an adult. The real estate scene was happening. Lots of us would go to the bars, the really nice ones, on our expense accounts, and drink and dance, and sometimes hook up."

"So Ashley could be any number of men's daughter."

She flushed again. "Oh my God. That sounds so awful."

"Why didn't you have a DNA test done? Prove he wasn't the father. I'm thinking that if you had proven Ashley wasn't his, he'd leave you alone. If she was his, you could go to court and solidify custody and get support from him."

She was silent. For a moment, I didn't think she was going to answer. Then she looked at me. "I thought I could control him. I thought I could use her as leverage. I underestimated him." She took a long shaky breath. "I tossed it up into his face. That she might not be his. I stupidly threw a name at him, of a realtor I had dated."

She was silent again. She buried her face in her hands and she began to cry. Blackhawk and I waited.

After a while she looked up, her face red and bloated. "A week later, the guy's boss called me, asking if I'd seen him. He'd not been to work for a week. No one knew where he was, he just disappeared." She shook her head. "Don had him killed. They never found him, but I know Don had him killed. I killed him."

I looked at Blackhawk He was looking at me.

Finally, I said, "You aren't telling us everything."

"What aren't you telling us?" Blackhawk said.

Again, she was silent. Thinking it through. Finally, she said, "When I heard Don's wife had cancer I thought I could push him to give me some money."

"In return for what?"

"In return for me not telling his wife about Ashley."

"Even though Ashley might not be his?"

"I told him she was."

I took a deep breath, took a big drink and leaned back. Blackhawk and I looked at each other.

All righty then.

41

I borrowed Nacho and Indigo. I knew that Tiger Lily and I were the only clues Newman had as to where Lindy and Ashley were. I knew they would show up sometime. We were all inside Thirteen Episodes. Pete handed out bottles of beer. Nacho sat on the couch with Indigo snuggled under his massive arm. Made me a little queasy. Like seeing your sister with a boyfriend. But we'd proven Indigo wasn't my sister. That didn't count, that was just curiosity on both sides, so the sister thing maybe seemed more appropriate now.

I had finished my explanation and Pete said, "So, you think they'll come back out here?"

Indigo took a drink and said "Duh."

"Be polite," Nacho said.

"Sorry, it's a habit of mine," Pete said. "Sometimes I'll repeat things out loud to give me an opportunity to think about it." He looked at me. "You've embarrassed them pretty good. They'll want their revenge."

"Counting on it," I said. "So, we wait. I've got Eddie up

at the bar. Maureen is keeping an eye out also. They both have my number." I looked at Pete. "I'd like to have Nacho and Indigo stay here, if that's okay."

"Sure," he said.

"And," I continued, "since they are the two horniest people on the planet, you might want to come down and bunk with me."

Nacho just grinned.

I stood up. I unzipped the duffel bag and pulled the two Mossbergs out. I set out four boxes of shells. Indigo still had her Beretta, I just couldn't tell where. I zipped the duffle and picked it up. Pete followed me out the door onto the bow.

I leaned back in. "The decent thing to do, will be to wash the sheets before you leave."

Indigo gave me the finger.

I stepped aboard the Lily and went through the sliding bow doors. I set the duffle on my long yellow couch and unpacked the rest of the weapons onto my coffee table. I slipped a holster onto my belt and situated it on my right hip. I checked the loads on the Kahr .45, and slipped it into the holster. I was wearing a chambray shirt over my tee shirt, untucked to hide the pistol.

"What should I use?" Pete said.

I shook my head. "You're the lawyer. I don't expect I'll have to use any firearm, I expect to intimidate. If it comes to gun play, which I will do everything in my power to prevent, but if it does, you duck in here and get as low as possible. You said you had business cards?"

"Yeah," he said. He pulled his wallet from his khaki

trousers and fished a card out. It read Ahern, Duffey and Dunn with a California P.O. Box address. I handed it back.

"These guys still practice law?"

He smiled. "Ahern died ten years ago, Duffey is retired and living someplace in Montana and I'm here."

"You never did tell me how that Western went."

"Too many chefs spoil the pot. Or, in this case, plot."

I didn't have any idea how long we would have to wait, so I took my toolbox up top to put on a new brass plate in the cockpit. Pete found a Jeff Shaara he hadn't read yet and settled on the couch. As it turned out, we didn't have to wait long. I was setting the screws when my phone startled me by vibrating in my pocket. I keep forgetting I have the damn thing.

I pulled it out. It was Eddie.

"Hi ho," he said. "You have company."

"Thanks," I said. I moved around toward the bow. They were coming through the gate onto the dock. There were three of them. One was older, heavier with silver white hair. Must be Newman. Then I saw the fourth one hustling along, over on Dock B. He was carrying a long blue duffel bag. I didn't have to guess what was in it.

I disconnected Eddie and thumbed the speed dial for Indigo. She answered, sounding out of breath.

"Yeah?"

"They are here. I have a bogy over on B Dock. He's carrying."

"Shit, right now? Really?"

I disconnected.

I stood on the top and watched them come. Halfway down the dock I saw them notice me. The big florid guy I'd dumped in the drink was beside Newman. He said something, and I watched Newman look up toward me.

I went down the winding stairs, through the stateroom and into the galley. I opened a cabinet and snagged a small Tupperware container. Pete looked up. "They're here," I said. "Stay in here until I call for you." Placing the container into my pocket, I stepped out on the bow, then onto the dock. I stood easily, waiting.

They walked by Thirteen Episodes. Nacho had battened it down. The curtains were drawn. I knew Nacho and his Mossberg were watching them parade by. Down the dock toward the gate, Indigo had boat hopped, and now stepped into sight, off of a Starliner, and onto the dock. She went through the gate and headed for Dock B.

Newman's face was impassive. The big guy had a scowl. It didn't make him any better looking.

They came to a halt in front of me. The big guy pulled his jacket back to show me his gun. Newman was studying me.

"I appreciate a good Seventh Day Adventist," I said. "You can leave your pamphlets if you wish."

"I don't need your lip," Newman said. "I want my girl."

I looked at him for a ten count. I wanted him to know I wasn't intimidated. "If you mean Ashley, she's not here."

"Tell me where she is, or you are going to get fucked up real bad."

"Really bad," I said. "I think it should be 'really bad'."

The big guy moved to bring his pistol out. I held up a finger, "Uh, before you do that, I'd look back there." I looked behind him.

"Bullshit," he said, pulling the gun.

Nacho pumped a shell into the Mossberg. The guy froze, and Newman turned to look. Newman then looked across to B Dock. His guy was standing in the sunlight, his hands behind his head. Indigo had her Beretta pointed at his head.

The big guy followed Newman's eyes. "Jesus," he said under his breath.

Newman looked back at me. "You don't know who you are fucking with."

I smiled. "No sir. It's the other way around. You don't know who you are fucking with." I nodded toward Indigo. "That woman over there is one of the most highly trained operatives our government ever had. You think you have connections? You think you and your mob buddies are tough because you think you can shoot us any time you wish. Ambush us from a dark alley. Take us down to the river and dump our bodies?"

"Yeah, that's what I think," Newman said.

"Let me give you an idea of what you are up against. We have the ability to take over your life. We can destroy any business you are a part of. Avalon? Sussex. Any business. We can make you disappear. Not just your body, which we can dump in the river bottom any time we want, but we can destroy any evidence that you were even on this planet. You think you are safe in Vegas? You think your mob buddies will protect you? We can be in your house and up your ass anytime we want. Guards, alarms, it doesn't matter. Or, if we want to be nice, and leave you alive, we can just ruin your reputation. You ever been a child molester? We can put it on the internet, or on the local TV. Yeah, everyone in Vegas will see your face, with the words 'Child Molester' plastered all over it."

He was watching me, his eyes were narrowed, but he didn't say anything. I stared at him for a very long moment.

I turned my head toward the boat, "Mr. Dunn."

Pete stepped out.

"Mr. Newman meet Mr. Dunn. Mr. Dunn is Ashley's attorney. Here's the way it is going to go. You have no evidence that Ashley is your daughter, except Lindy told you she was. Well, Lindy told Mr. Dunn and me that you aren't the father. But she has no evidence. So what Mr. Dunn wants is a sample to be tested for a match with Ashley's DNA."

I fished the Tupperware from my pocket and held it out to him. He looked at it. "What the fuck is that?"

"I need you to pee in that," Pete said. "To go to the lab."

"You are out of your fucking mind," he said, his face reddening.

"Are you saying you refuse to allow a DNA test?" I said.

"I ain't pissing in that damn thing," he said.

I punched him in the nose. A straight smack with a twist at the end. It was a good one. He staggered back, then went to one knee. Blood ran down his chin. The big guy was not quick, and Nacho had the barrel of the shotgun against the back of his neck before he could move. The other guy was frozen. I leaned forward and grabbed Newman by the hair. I placed the Tupperware under his nose and caught a few drops of blood. Enough.

"I don't need piss. Blood will do."

I stepped back and put the lid back onto the container and handed it to Pete. Newman was struggling to his feet. I pulled a handkerchief from my back pocket and handed it to him. He took it and wadded it against his nose. I'm guessing he'd not been punched in a long time. Maybe never.

"You broke my nose," he said. It was muffled against the cloth and sounded like, "You oke my node."

"I didn't really want to watch you piss in the cup. You take your amateur hour thugs back to Vegas, Mr. Newman, and we will be in touch. If Ashley is yours, Mr. Dunn will meet with your attorneys and work out what arrangements are appropriate. If Ashley isn't yours, you will never be in contact with her or her mother again. We will be watching. If you try to retaliate in any way, toward me or toward the girl, or toward the girl's mother, the first thing we'll do is smear Vegas with your picture and fact that you are a child molester. If you persist, I will have you killed."

"Child molester? I ain't no child molester."

"You will be if I say you are."

I turned and waved at Indigo. She began marching her guy back down the dock.

"Go now," I said.

Without a word, Newman turned, and they went past Nacho and back down the dock.

216

Pete and I watched them until they went through the gate. The big guy turned to look back at me, but he didn't stop walking. Pete said, "Jesus, Jackson. Aren't you afraid of anything?"

"Commitment," I said.

42

It was two days later. Lindy and Ashley were still at Blackhawk and Elena's apartment. Ashley had fallen head over heels for Elena, and vice versa. Blackhawk and I were sitting in his office, standing at the two-way window watching the happy hour crowd below.

"You think you've scared that Newman guy off?" Blackhawk said.

"No," I said.

"Me neither," he said.

We stood watching some more. Nacho was helping Jimmy behind the bar and Indigo sat in Nacho's regular stool, reading.

"I like to watch people read," I said.

"You are one weird dude. But, it's like I heard you say."

"What?"

"People that don't read only experience one lonely life."

I smiled. "I would never know what it would be like to be a one-legged sea captain sailing the high seas if I hadn't read Moby Dick. What have you read lately?"

"I read those Steinbeck books you put me onto. Cannery Row and Sweet Thursday."

"What'd you think?"

"Things were simpler then. But I could see us with Mack and the boys."

I chuckled.

"So what do we do?" he continued.

"About Newman?"

"Yeah, about Newman."

"I've been thinking about that."

"And?"

"We need to prove that my threats are not just threats."

"What do you have in mind?"

"Two things. One, we go to Vegas and show him we can do what I said we can do. Including hacking the man and show him we can spread lies about him all over cyberspace."

"Or, the truth."

"Yeah, or the truth. At least show him we can do it."

Blackhawk thought about that. "I don't like the idea of getting Jimmy's friend involved in this stuff. I think we need a pro."

I went over to the couch and sat down. "So, you thinking what I'm thinking?"

He sat behind his desk. "What are you thinking?"

"Call the colonel, get the old gang together."

"What are you, Andy fucking Hardy?"

"If you'll be my Judy Garland. We can go out to the barn and put on a show."

43

Martha answered the phone.

"Hello, ma'am, it's Jackson."

"Why Jackson. So good to hear from you." As usual it was like talking to your grandmother. Always warm and friendly. I knew her, and the colonel had retired to the southern part of Illinois, but I hadn't been there. So in my mind's eye I always saw her in a farm kitchen with a gingham apron, talking on an old party-line crank telephone on the wall.

"I trust you are well, ma'am."

"Old age, Jackson. My advice is, don't do it. But of course not everyone gets the opportunity, so I suppose I shouldn't complain. The colonel is in the other room. Hold on, I'll get him."

"Thank you, ma'am."

After a few moments I heard him pick up the phone. "Hello Jackson," he said in that deep baritone of his..

"Hello, sir."

"I'm sure you are calling to enquire about my rheumatism and my knee surgery."

"Yes sir. How are your rheumatism and your knee?"

"Just fine, Jackson. They are just fine. Now, what can I do for you?"

"I'm trying to help a young woman and her seven-year-old daughter. I could use some help."

"Tell me about it."

So I did.

As usual he didn't interrupt. When I finished, he was silent a long time. I waited.

"So you threatened this guy and now you want to make good on it."

"Pretty much."

"The guy's a civilian. As tough and scary as he thinks he is, he really isn't."

"No sir, he isn't."

"This may cost you some money. Nobody works for free anymore. Except for, maybe the good Samaritans, you and Blackhawk. And did I hear you say Indigo is with you?"

"Yes, sir."

"And you ran into her by accident?"

"Yes sir."

"I don't believe in coincidence," he said. "Are you sure it was coincidental?"

"It's been a while, and I haven't seen anything to the contrary. She's fallen in lust with a friend of mine."

"Yes, of course she has." He paused again. "I have a young woman that has done work for me that has a really remarkable ability with cyber-technology. You figure out what you want and when. She will cost you a thousand. For the other, I can contact Echo and Fabian. They should be available, unless they have taken side jobs. That would give you a five-man team. That should be enough. What will you pay?"

"I was hoping five-hundred a man. I pay all expenses for no more than two days in Vegas. They'll gamble it away at the airport, on their way out of town anyway."

He chuckled. "Most likely. I'll run it by them. Have them call this number?"

"Yes sir."

"Very well. Come see us sometime, Jackson. Martha would love to see you. We aren't getting any younger." He disconnected. The conversation was over.

44

I booked three rooms, double queens, at Circus Circus for $49 a night. Two-night minimum. They were all on the same floor. Blackhawk, Indigo and I flew in on an early bird Southwest flight. Indigo almost had to fist-fight Nacho to keep him from coming.

Echo was coming in from Seattle, and Fabian was coming from Chicago. Both were due in at about the same time, around, five o'clock. We had the day to wait. Indigo went to the pool, to work on her tan. Blackhawk and I rented a van, with cash and a clean, but bogus, credit card. We drove out to see Newman's property.

We each had hard-copy satellite imaging of the surrounding area, showing all the streets and main thoroughfares. We spent a couple of hours driving into, and then out of, his posh neighborhood. Timing it to the freeways, then timing it to the airport. This was just precautionary, but we had been taught to do our due diligence.

The guy's property was impressive. A large, almost ten-thousand square-foot, terracotta tiled roof mansion. It was enclosed in a fenced, five-acre compound that was surrounded by ocotillos, bougainvillea and palm trees. It was in an area that proudly called itself Seven Bridges. I saw no bridges. On the other side of the gate was a U-shaped drive that, at its apex, had a two-car garage on each side of the covered entry between. As we went by, Blackhawk took pictures of the vehicles parked in front and of the two guards that were in the guard shack at the gate. We drove around the block, if you wanted to call it that. It was more like driving around a small farm. There was a canal bordering the back. That made it a little more problematic. The good news was that, as rich as this area was, there wasn't an HOA wall or gate and guard to contend with. Each property stood alone. Most were gated on their own.

Satisfied, we drove back to Circus Circus, stopping at a grocery where we bought a bottle of Wild Turkey and a bottle of Smirnoffs, along with chips and nuts and such. We drove back and parked in the casino garage. We still had a little time to kill so we went to the casino to gamble. I wasn't crazy about gambling, but it passed the time.

At half past five we were back in our room when Indigo knocked. I let her in.

"Bottle's on the dresser," I said.

She fixed a drink and sat by the window. She looked out the window. "Place is a shithole," she said.

"You would know," Blackhawk said. "You worked here." She didn't reply. She took a drink.

Blackhawk and I fixed a drink and dragged chairs over by her. We sat, put our feet up on the air unit that was under the window and sipped our drinks. We were quiet as we waited. Finally, there was a knock on the door,

I looked out the peep hole. It was Echo and Fabian. Echo was a smaller, slender and dark guy. Head of thick black hair. Stronger and tougher than he looked. Fabian looked like his code name. Coiffed hair, a little long over the ears. Good looking, like a TV stud. About my size, with a ready smile. Liked to joke. Knew when not to joke. Steady in action. Reliable. I opened the door.

Blackhawk and Indigo didn't get up. It wasn't that kind of reunion.

I stepped back to let them in. "Glasses, ice and booze on the dresser," I said.

"Circus Circus, for Christ's sake," Fabian said, fixing his drink. "I expected the Bellagio or at least the Wynn."

"You always did have champagne tastes," Indigo said.

"I only have a beer budget," I said. I sat on the bed, leaving my chair for one of them. "I appreciate you coming. Get your drink and I'll tell you what we have."

Once we were all settled, I said, "Did the colonel give you any background?"

They both shook their head. "He said you'd fill us in," Fabian said. "Just said it's a two-day job and you're good for a K."

"Half a K," I said, "but nice try."

"Half a K," he said, with a grin.

"In a nutshell, here it is. I have an asshole, a made guy that is bothering a friend of mine. A friend with a seven-year-old daughter. She was this jerk's girlfriend at one time.

She got pregnant, and she made the mistake of telling the guy the baby was his. She tells me she lied. She was just trying to leverage him. But now the guy says he wants the little girl. At any rate I want this jerk out of her life. I explained to him…"

"As you punched him in the nose," Indigo grinned.

"Yeah, as I punched him in the nose, what we could do to him, if he didn't walk out of their lives. And stay out."

"And this girl is just a friend?" Fabian said, looking at me with a half-smile.

"She was abandoned with the girl and no money, so she comes knocking on Jackson's door," Indigo said.

"I thought you lived on a boat," Echo said.

"Boats have doors," I said.

"Why do you care?" Fabian said.

"Because he came on my dock and threatened my guest," I said.

"You always did want to joust with windmills," Echo said.

"So you threatened him, and you don't think he believes you."

"No," Blackhawk said. "He *doesn't* believe us. This is a bad guy. He's not above killing the woman to get the child. In the civilian world he is a very scary guy. And he is used to getting whatever he wants. He's got the mob behind him and a punch in the nose just pissed him off."

"So you want to show him what scary really is," Echo said.

"Yeah, pretty much. I want him to know we can reach

out and tweak his nose any time we want."

"So we go tweak his nose?"

"Jesus Christ," Indigo said. "Where do you get this nursery rhyme shit? Tweak his nose."

"What would *you* say?" Blackhawk said, smiling.

"I'd scare the little fucker until he shit his pants."

Fabian laughed. "I like her version."

Blackhawk stood and went to the dresser. He opened a drawer and pulled a stack of papers. There were five packets, each stapled together. He handed them out.

"These are the schematics on the house. One shows the floor plan. The other the grounds. Then the third one shows the street grid of the roads around the place. In the back are photos we took of the house, vehicles and guards." He looked at Echo. "You get the security system." He handed Echo a blueprint. "As you see, it's not that complicated. People that believe they are scary can't imagine someone coming into their lair."

"Lair?" Indigo said.

He ignored her. "The weakness to the electronic security is there is only one power source, with no back-up. Not even batteries." He leaned over and touched Echo's blueprint. "Here, at the back, and the main out by the street."

Echo studied it. "The guy's an idiot."

"Yeah, he is," said Blackhawk. "But we don't go in thinking that. We go in thinking he is as big and bad and scary as he thinks he is."

"We don't go in over-confident," I said.

"When do we go?" Fabian said.

"I'm planning early in the morning. Say about four o'clock. I'm waiting for a text from the colonel on another surprise we'll have for the guy."

"What kind of surprise?' Fabian said.

"I'll show you when we are in and have the guy. You're going to like it."

"What about tools?" Echo said. He meant firearms and such.

"The colonel arranged to have them in our rental van this afternoon. They're probably already there. It cost me a couple of grand."

"So you think this broad is worth this, and she's only a friend?"

"She's only a friend," Indigo said.

"It's not the woman," I said. "The little one is worth it. This asshole stays in her life, it will fuck her up."

"What do we do with the guy once we have him?" Echo said.

"Indigo will make him shit his pants," Blackhawk said.

45

At three fifteen in the morning we were at the van, changing our clothes. The clothes we changed into were worthy of a SWAT team. Dark clothes, rubber-soled shoes, ski masks, Kevlar vests, and even helmets. The weapons were used, but they worked. Two shotguns, five pistols, all loaded. No extra shells. All were expendable. They would be ditched when we finished.

Blackhawk drove. We pulled up to the guard shack at four. There was only one guard at night. He had been watching a little TV but was asleep when Indigo and Fabian hit him. They trussed him up with duct tape and swung the gate open just before Echo shut down the security system and cut the power. Indigo whispered to the guard that if he put his head outside the shack she would blow it off.

They piled back in and Blackhawk drove up to the door. Without security lights, the place was pitch black. Amazing, no battery backup, nothing. I had covered the lens of my combat light so that only a sliver of light came through. I put the sliver on the lock and Echo pulled his small packet of tools and popped the door in less than thirty seconds.

We went in silently. The house was quiet. As planned, Indigo and Fabian went up the circular stairway that was to our left. The upstairs had a game room, a media room complete with recliners and a popcorn machine, and three bedrooms. They were goon hunting. Blackhawk and Echo took the family room and the small bedroom that bracketed the dining area. I went through the living room, into the vestibule to the master suite. The door was closed. I tested the knob and it turned.

I silently slid the door open. There were two massive walk-ins on either side. It was too dark to see. I flashed the light into a walk-in for a second. Newman's bed was against the far wall and there was a lump in the middle of it. He was alone. There was a bed stand on the left side. I silently went to it, flicking the light a second at a time, pointed at the floor. I opened the drawer. He had his 9 mm Taurus in it. I gently took it out. I went to the foot of his bed and sat down. He groaned but didn't wake.

I pulled the electrical tape from my light. I wadded the tape and put it into my pocket. I shined the light into his face. I held it there for at least thirty seconds before he moved. Suddenly he sat up, putting his hand out to block the light.

"What the hell," he said.

I stood up. "Get up," I said.

"What the fuck? Who is it?"

I walked around and hit him in the head with his pistol. Just enough to draw blood, but not enough to put him out.

"Get up," I said again.

"Son of a bitch," he said. He put his hand to his head, then looked at the bloody hand.

I moved toward him again. He thrust his hand out. "Wait, wait." He climbed off the bed and came to his feet. He slept in pajamas.

"We're going downstairs," I said.

"Who the fuck are you?"

"Downstairs," I said, drawing my hand back to hit him again.

"Wait, wait," he said again. He started moving. I kept the light on him, so he could see to walk.

"Into the living room," I said.

When we got there, the party was complete. There were four guys standing in their underwear, their hands zip tied behind them.

"Put the power on," I said to Echo. He went out the front door. A few seconds later the power came on and he came back in. Blackhawk switched on a couple of lights. I put the combat light away.

"What the fuck is this?" Newman said.

"Shut up," Indigo said. Newman started, surprised she was a woman. You couldn't tell by looking. She looked at Fabian. "Put those two armchairs side by side. Leave about four feet between them." Fabian complied. She turned back to Newman. "Take your jammies off."

"What the fuck are you talking about?" He was getting his bluster back.

Indigo turned and shot one of his men in the thigh. The

man screamed and fell to the floor. "Take your jammies off," she said.

Newman stared at her. She waved her pistol at him, but he still just stared at her. She turned and shot another one in the leg. He howled and went down. She turned to Newman. "Take your jammies off or you are next."

Newman slowly started to slip out of his pajamas. We all knew that there is something psychologically debilitating to be naked in front of your enemies. It takes the bluster right out of you. You can be brave and stubborn all day long, but once you are naked in front of strangers, especially bad guy strangers, all that goes away.

He got down to his tighty whities, when she said "Stop. I don't want to see your frizzled little pecker." She waved the pistol at the two chairs. "Go stand between the chairs." Newman moved over and stood between the chairs.

"Now, squat down between them."

He started to go down on his knees.

"No, not on your knees, squat down." Newman squatted. She looked at Fabian, "Zip his wrists to the arms of the chairs. One at the wrist, one at the elbow. Make them tight."

Fabian pulled out two black zip ties and did as she asked. I looked at Blackhawk and he looked at me. Neither of us had a clue as to what she was doing.

Once Newman was secure, Fabian stepped back. Indigo went to Newman and squatted down so their faces were on the same level. She reached over and pulled the elastic of his underwear. She shoved her pistol down there and said,

"Now, I want you to shit your pants. If you don't, I'm going to blow your dick off."

Newman began to breath heavy, his face red in full blown panic.

"Do it now," Indigo said calmly.

"I can't," he cried. "I can't."

She pulled the hammer back on the pistol and Newman literally began to cry. "I can't, I can't."

Indigo stayed looking at him for a long time. Now he was gasping for breath, ragged and sobbing. She finally stood up. She looked at me. "I tried," she said.

I nodded. I looked at Echo. "Turn the TV on," I said. He found the remote and switched it on. I pulled my phone. "Put it on CNN," I said. Echo found the channel. "Turn the volume up a little," I said. He did. I pressed the pre-determined speed dial code on my phone.

I looked at Newman. "You'll want to watch this," I said.

After a few seconds, there was a blip on the screen, then Newman's face appeared. The photo was an old booking photo, but it was unmistakably Newman. A woman's voice came over the photo. "*This is an amber alert. This man is being sought for kidnapping a young girl after sexually molesting her. His name is Donald Newman and he is wanted for many counts of child molestation and child pornography. If you see this man, notify your local authorities immediately.*" Her voice stopped, but the photo lingered. Finally, she said, "*He is considered dangerous. And now back to our regularly scheduled programming.*" There was a blip and the regular show continued.

I looked at Newman. He was defeated and deflated. "You

have been warned." I pulled the manila envelope from my shirt. I opened it and took out the official looking document Pete had put together for me.

I tossed it on the chair. "These are the official results of the DNA test for you and the girl, using your own blood. There is no match. You are not related."

I walked over to him and squatted down, putting my face inches from his. I stared at him for a long while. He looked everywhere except at me. "If you, or anyone working for you, comes within ten miles of that little girl or her mother, we will come back." I stood. "I know in a couple of days you'll get your courage back and you'll start thinking about revenge. If you try to act on that, you will be killed."

I looked at Fabian. "Cut his right hand loose." Fabian leaned down and cut the zip ties. I took out a pen and a small notebook. I put them on the chair. "You have an associate by the name of Bill that is associated with Sussex Financial. He's the guy that supplied the girls for your parties. I want you to write down everything you know about him. Name, address, phone, everything. If you don't, I will have the woman shoot you in the balls."

"My pleasure," Indigo said.

He took the pen and began writing. When he finished, he croaked, "That's all I know."

I looked at it. I put the notebook and pen in my pocket. I looked at Blackhawk and nodded toward the door. We went out, piled into the van and drove away.

As we pulled the ski masks off, Indigo said, "So that dirt bag isn't related to Ashley at all?"

I looked out the window. "I have no idea."

46

Full circle. Blackhawk and I were sitting at the slots in the Verde River Casino. We were watching a medium-sized guy on a stool, with a big guy standing behind him, cheating a slot machine. They were in the row ahead of us using an emp jammer. Stick it up the machine's kazoo and disrupt the signals and pull in the cash. The big guy was a shield, hoovering over the other guy, blocking the view of fellow gamblers and more importantly, the security cameras. The place was half empty. It was a weekday, but it was still noisy. Like all casinos are noisy. Clackity clack, ding ding, bingity bong. Every once in a while, the bells would ring, indicating a winner.

Lindy came and sat at the empty machine between us. She leaned over and hugged Blackhawk.

"Thank you so much," she said.

"You got it?" I said.

"I got the job," she smiled.

Blackhawk and Elena, primarily Elena, had gotten Lindy an interview with Tomas Marino, the casino manager, for a mid-level job in his organization.

"Happy to help," Blackhawk said.

"You all moved in?" I said.

"Yep, and Ashley started her first day in second grade today. She loves her teacher."

"She loves everyone."

"Yes, she does."

She looked at me, going solemn. "You sure we won't be bothered by Don again?"

"I can't absolutely guarantee anything. But, I'm 99.9% sure this guy won't want to bother you again."

"What did you do?"

I looked across at Blackhawk. He smiled. "Jackson reasoned with him," he said.

"Indigo helped him see the light," I said.

Lindy nodded. "I like her," she said. "But I have to admit, she scares me sometimes."

"She can be scary," I said. "But she's on our side."

Blackhawk pulled his phone and punched a number in. In a moment he said, "Big guy and his buddy in front of us. They have a jammer." He listened, then disconnected. In just a few moments a team of security moved in on the two guys. The guy with the jammer didn't even have time to get it back in his bag. They jerked him off his stool and marched him away. The big guy gave no resistance. The guys on the security team were as big as he was.

Lindy was watching, wide eyed. "Wow, what did they do?"

"Cheating," I said. I slid off my stool. "I'm hungry," I

said. "Suppose Mr. Marino would spring for a steak dinner?"

"I'm sure Mr. Marino would," Blackhawk said. "And they have great prime rib here."

"And," I said, "I want to talk to you both about William S. Hesse."

"Who's that?" Lindy said, following me.

"He's the Bill guy you said brought the girls to Newman's party."

"How do you know that?" She looked at Blackhawk. "How do you guys know this stuff?"

"I'll tell you all about it over a cocktail and a steak," I said. Of course, I didn't. No wizard worth his salt shows you what's behind the curtain.

47

It was a week later. Elena was on a remodel kick. She had been watching a popular remodel show on the tube and it gave her the bug. Indigo was showing an unusual streak of the domestics, and was enthusiastically joining in. Blackhawk and Nacho had escaped, and we were up top of the Tiger Lily, in the shade of the cockpit canopy, drinking Dos Equis.

"So, how do we get to this Hesse guy?" Blackhawk said.

"Someone has to pay for Nikki and Simone," Nacho said, watching the lake.

"Yes, they do," I said. "We need to get him arrested. Sex traffickers, especially those trading in young girls, don't do well in the big house."

"In the big house?" Blackhawk said, looking at me. "What are you? Broderick Crawford?"

"Who's Broderick Crawford?" Nacho said.

"Before your time," I said.

"Before *your* time," Blackhawk said to me.

I nodded. "Yea, but you know if I did have a TV, I'd

probably waste my days away watching those old black and white movies. You know, Bette Davis, Dick Powell, Humphrey Bogart, those guys."

"Don't know any of them," Nacho said.

"Your loss," I said. He shrugged.

"What we know," I said, "is what the girls told us. The organization good ole Luis was in, was Southwest and Vegas and West coast and huge."

"Luis is gone," Blackhawk said. "Who's the new Luis?"

"Good question."

"Find the new Luis and get him to lead us to Hesse. Set him up somehow."

"How do we find out who it is?" I said.

Nacho made a noise in his throat as he took a long pull on the beer.

We both looked at him. He swallowed, then leaning back, let out a long low belch. It seemed to go on and on.

When he finished he said, "We could ask."

"Mouths of babes," Blackhawk said.

"Ask who?" I said.

He turned slightly to look at me. "You showed me a list of strip clubs that asshole Luis was hooked up with. Whoever took his spot would pick up where he left off."

"True that."

"I could go nose around. See if I can come up with a name."

"Mendoza," I said.

Nacho looked at me like I was crazy. "It ain't Mendoza."

"No, what I mean is Mendoza could ask Vice if they have

anything, either on Luis's replacement or on Hesse himself. Maybe check with Vegas Vice, professional courtesy. When can you start hitting the strip clubs?"

"No time like the present," he said. Sitting his empty down. He got up and went down the stairway.

"He just likes looking at the titties," Blackhawk said.

The next morning I was sitting in the waiting area, out in the hallway, down from Mendoza's new office. I was sitting with a good assortment of dirtbags waiting to answer for the dirtbag stuff they had done.

Across from me was Mr. Jitters. Strung out, skin and bones, long greasy hair, looked like the typical user. But the good news was, he was old enough to vote.

He leaned toward me. "Hey, buddy. You got a cigarette?"

"Don't smoke," I said.

"You don't smoke?" he said. He said it like it was the most outrageous thing he'd ever heard.

"There's no smoking here anyway," I said.

"No smoking?" Again, with the outrage. He glared at me for a while. Finally, he said, "You got any change?"

This time I shifted and looked directly at him. "Shut the fuck up, or I will bounce your head against the wall until your eyes fall out."

He started to say something, then thought better of it. He turned away. I settled back and waited. After a while, Detective Armstead came and got me. Armstead was Mendoza's driver and body man now that Mendoza had been promoted.

I followed his broad back to Mendoza's office. He was

starting to sport a thin spot on the crown of his head. I suppose my turn will come.

He waved me into the empty office. "The captain is in a meeting. He would like you to wait." I nodded my thanks and he went away.

The office was like Mendoza, spotless, neat and efficient. I sat in one of the two chairs that fronted his desk. I pushed it back, stretched my legs out and waited. I'd been taught to wait. To not move, hardly breathe and wait. The longer I've been out, and the older I get, the harder it is.

Finally, I heard him behind me and I sat up and turned. He was in his shirt sleeves, but still looked starched and neat. His tie was up and tight, his trousers pressed with a sharp crease down each leg, his shirt collar starched and white. He came around me and sat in his chair. He didn't offer to shake hands. I'd probably fall over if he did.

He had a sheaf of papers in his hand. He laid them on his desk and looked through them. I waited. Finally, he looked up. He leaned back in his chair and it creaked. "So, Jackson. What can I help you with? I know you're going to ask something, so let's get to it. I have a busy morning."

"Good to see you too, sir." He just looked at me, waiting. Okay then. "There is a large sex trade organization operating here, Vegas and on the West coast."

He cocked his head. "This involves you how?"

"I became acquainted with two young women recently. Friends of a friend. They both were a part of this organization."

"They were prostitutes."

241

I nodded. "They were both murdered by the organization. One you know about. At least Detective Boyce knows about her. The other, you don't know about. Her body was dumped in the city dump. Her body will never be found."

"Names?"

"The names they gave me were Simone Dove and Nikki Boyd."

He studied me for a minute. "Simone Dove's real name was Emily Sykes. I haven't heard of the other one."

"Luis Portofino was the pimp that ran the local organization. He was the one that had them killed."

He leaned forward and tented his fingers. "Luis Portofino has disappeared," he said. "Do you know anything about that?"

"No, except good riddance. What I do know is that the entire organization is run by a guy name of William S. Hesse."

I noticed he didn't take notes. He probably knew a hell of a lot more than I did.

"So, like I said, what is it I can help you with?"

"This guy deals in little girls. Younger the better. It offends me. I want to take him down."

"That would be Vice. I'm the Homicide Commander."

"I don't know anyone in Vice," I said. "I know you."

"Lucky me," he said.

48

Two nights later we were at the El Patron. Elena wasn't performing, so the bar was slow. Captain Mendoza said he would get back to me. Usually, when someone tells me that, I'm a little skeptical. But this was Mendoza. He always did what he said he would do. Sometimes, you might not want him to, but he always did it.

I was nursing a second beer. Sometimes I get bored with beer, so sometimes I'll try something new. Tonight, it was something called a *Kiltlifter*. This was an image I wasn't fond of. The beer was okay, but I'm just bored with beer. I had a long drive back to the boat, so I didn't want anything stronger. I was mulling my fate when I saw Jimmy lift his head and break into a large smile. I swiveled on my stool and Detective First Grade Boyce was walking into the room. She was dressed the way she usually dressed, dark slacks, dark jacket and crisp white blouse. Her badge wasn't on her belt. She must be off duty. The pistol was still on her hip, under the jacket. It was never off duty.

She slid up on the stool next to me.

"The sign out front says, 'no firearms allowed,'" I said.

"Fuck the sign," she said. Jimmy came up and set a coaster in front of her.

"What'll it be, Detective?" he said.

"Jimmy, make me one of your great Grey Goose martinis," she said.

"Coming up," he said. He looked at me. "Another beer?"

"Ballantine's on the rocks," I said. To hell with it.

I swiveled to look at her. She was looking at the empty bandstand. "Elena's not singing tonight?"

"Now that's good detecting, took the night off," I said. "Even multi-lingual superstars take a night off now and then."

She looked at me. "You always have to say something cute?"

"It's a gift," I said.

"That unfortunately keeps on giving," she said.

Jimmy brought the drinks. I lifted my rock glass. She reached over and clinked it, then took a drink. Okay, progress toward detente.

"The captain says you are interested in William S. Hesse?"

"Yes," I said.

"Why?" she said.

"You sent me a picture of a dead girl," I said. "A blonde girl."

"Yes, Emily Sykes."

"I knew her as Simone Dove."

"AKA," she said. She took another drink. This one was more like a bird peck.

"Probably. I have no doubt that Hesse had her killed. I've told Mendoza…"

"Captain Mendoza," she said.

"Captain Mendoza," I repeated. "That there was another one. We knew her as Nikki Boyd. They shot her and dumped her body in a dumpster at a strip joint on Union Hills and Cave Creek Road. Once the body goes to the landfill, they'll never find her. Doesn't matter. I know she's dead. I want this Hesse guy to pay."

"You know this how?"

I shook my head. She looked at me hard, for a long time.

Finally, she said, "You know what obstruction of justice is?"

"Yeah," I said. "It's what politicians do before breakfast."

She resumed looking at me. Finally, she said, "I'm not going to fight you on this. The captain asked me to tell you what we know."

I took a drink and nodded.

"Hesse is the head of a large prostitution organization. It's like a corporation, got offices in Los Angeles, Vegas, Phoenix, Reno and Albuquerque. There is a federal task force that has had him on the radar for quite a while. But he's smart. He has several layers of insulation between him and the actual dirty work. They, so far, haven't been able to touch him." She looked at me. "What do you know about him?"

"Just what I told you," I said, "which isn't much."

"What do you know about Luis Portofino?"

I shook my head. "Who?"

She had hitched around and was looking at me steadily.

"He headed Hesse's outfit here. Running girls out of strip clubs. Including the one you just mentioned. He disappeared. You know anything about that?"

"Nope. Who's in charge now?"

"You don't know anything about him, but you want to know who's replacing him?"

"Yep."

"We don't know," she said, finishing her martini in one gulp. "Yet." She set the glass on the bar.

There was movement behind me and I turned. Nacho sat at the bar across from us. He smiled big at Boyce. "Good afternoon, Detective," he said.

She nodded at him. "Nacho."

She slid off her stool and looked at me. "The captain wants you to keep him informed of anything you find. That okay with you?"

"Of course," I said. She walked out. Nacho and I both watched her until she went through the double doors. A world class exit. Damn.

Nacho and I looked at each other. Blackhawk came down the stairs and slid up onto the stool Boyce had just vacated.

"You find anything?" he said to Nacho.

"Yeah," he said. "Word is Luis's replacement is a woman."

"A woman?" I said.

He nodded, "Yep."

"Got a name?" Blackhawk said.

"Got a first name," he said. "Bartender said her name is Julie."

"Julie!" Blackhawk and I said simultaneously, looking at each other.

49

All the next week, Nacho and Indigo went on a fact-finding tour of the strip clubs that had been on Luis's list. It was tricky gathering information without gathering suspicion. They found the best sources of information were from the girls themselves. Evidently, Julie's transition into the Phoenix scene had not been seamless. One pimp had purportedly ended up dead. But there was no proof because there was no body. Two others had broken bones to speed along their cooperation.

Julie's name was Wang.

"As in Wang's wing," I said. Everyone just looked at me. "You know, like in *Murder by Death*." They all just shook their heads and turned away. "You know, Peter Falk, Alec Guinness."

They still wouldn't look at me. They started talking about something else.

"Peter Sellars," I kept trying. Nope.

"The word is," Nacho was saying, "Julie Wang is from Vegas, but she has moved here. She's run by the mob out of L.A."

"It's pretty common knowledge with the girls that the old boss was killed. But they say nobody could prove it," Indigo said. "One girl calls herself *Starbright*, yeah, no shit, says they are all nervous because the word is, two of the girls were killed at the same time."

"So, Julie Wang is in Phoenix now?" I said, to get back into this conversation.

"Starbright says Wang is just here to clean up a mess. Says she's higher up in the organization, so she's just here to right the ship."

"And the stripper knows this how?" Blackhawk said.

Indigo shrugged. "Says Wang told her this. Saying she didn't want to be here any longer than she has to be. Says Wang said she hated Phoenix."

"You find out where Wang is living?"

Nacho shook his head. "No one seems to know. But here's something. She is still recruiting. Told the girls she'll pay a thousand-dollar bonus to anyone that brings in a new girl that works out." He smiled, glancing at Indigo. "Starbright told Indigo she's too old."

It was hard, but Blackhawk and I didn't laugh.

"Bitch," Indigo said. "I'm tired of hearing that shit."

"A thousand bucks for a new girl, huh?" I thought about that. I pulled my phone and called Boyce.

The next day I met Boyce downtown in the bar of the legendary restaurant called the Stockyards. The bar took you back to the 1880's. It was all cowboy and western. It was great. I got there early and was enjoying a gin gimlet when Boyce came through the doors from the restaurant part. She slid into the booth beside me. The waitress was right there.

"What can I get you, ma'am," the young bright-eyed girl asked.

"Give me a cosmo, up, no fruit," she said.

The waitress looked at me, and I nodded. She went away to fill our order. Boyce was watching her.

"Ma'am," Boyce said, with a taste of distain. "Just when did I become a ma'am?"

"Always a fresh nymph to me," I said.

"Fuck you." She turned to look at me. "So, what is this all about?"

"Just drinks with an old friend," I said. She just looked at me.

Oh well, so much for banter. "Julie Wang," I said.

"Who's Julie Wang?"

"She is taking over from Luis Portofino."

"Thought you didn't know Luis Portofino."

I shrugged. "The mob boss in L.A. sent Julie Wang here to clean up the mess left by Portofino disappearing."

She started to speak, but the waitress was on her way back with our drinks. We were silent as she set them expertly before us. I thanked her, and she moved away.

"Okay," Boyce said, taking a sip. "I'll tell the captain. Better yet, I'll tell Vice."

"Okay," I said. "But I'd like a favor."

She took another sip, looking at me over the rim of the glass.

"I need a young girl."

She set her glass down. "I'll bet you do."

"A female cop that looks about twelve years old."

"That's young."

"Younger the better. Wang is offering a thousand-dollar bonus to any of her girls that recruit another girl that works out."

Boyce's eyebrows went up. "That's a lot."

"So, I'd like to wire up a girl and get her in with Julie Wang. If we can get Wang, we'll use her to get Hesse."

"You are an ambitious motherfucker," Boyce said. She shook her head, "Why don't you just leave this to Vice?"

"They'd just fuck it up. Besides, it's personal," I said.

"It always is for you." She finished her drink and signaled the waitress for another.

50

They were waiting for me in Mendoza's office. We had trouble finding a parking spot, so we were five minutes late. *We* were Blackhawk and me. Mendoza had extra chairs in his office, in our honor. He was behind his desk. Boyce had pulled a chair, so her back was against the wall. Another woman sat in one of the other chairs. I say woman, but she looked more like a kid. She was in uniform. She sat stiffly, with her best poker face on.

Mendoza waved to the other two chairs. We sat down. Mendoza looked at the patrolwoman, then back to me.

"Gentlemen, you know Detective Boyce. This is Officer Jane Marie Landers. Officer Landers is a patrol officer in our Maryvale Precinct." He waved a hand at me. "This is Jackson, and this gentleman," he indicated Blackhawk, "is Blackhawk."

Jane Marie nodded. She looked at me. "Mr. Jackson, what is your first name, if I might ask?"

Boyce and Mendoza looked at me.

"Jackson," I said.

"Oh. I'm sorry, I took that to be your last name."

"It is," I said.

"He's being an asshole," Boyce said.

Jane Marie looked at Blackhawk. "Just Blackhawk," he said with a smile. Jane Marie turned her eyes back to Mendoza.

Mendoza said, "Let's get to it. I have things to do." He looked at Boyce. "Did you explain things to Officer Landers?"

"Somewhat," she said. "This is Jackson's thing, I thought he should provide the details."

Mendoza looked at me. "Go ahead," he said.

I hitched around to look at Landers. "There is a billion-dollar sex trade organization operating here and in Nevada, New Mexico and California. Probably other places too. They operate out of strip clubs, private gambling clubs and sometimes at high end week-end parties. Sometimes the girls are flown on private jets to exotic locations for fun and games. Despite what it looks like on the surface, it is deadly, to the point where girls are murdered if they don't comply with the rules."

I looked at Blackhawk. "That about it?" He nodded.

"I need a girl," I continued, "to infiltrate. The girls in the strip clubs are being offered a thousand-dollar bonus to recruit new talent. Here in Phoenix, there has been some trouble with the management in the organization. The guy in charge, in California, name of William S. Hesse, has sent in a fixer to take care of the trouble. This fixer is named Julie Wang. She's the one offering the thousand dollars. I need you, or someone like you, to be recruited. We'll wire you up. We get Julie Wang, then we can get Hesse." I stopped to let this sink in. "Any questions?"

"How far in do I have to go?"

"If you get the Wang woman to be recorded explaining that you will be having sex for money with their customers, we have her," Mendoza said. "It must be explicit."

She was looking at Mendoza. "Is he a vice detective?" Meaning me.

Mendoza leaned back into his chair. He almost smiled. "He's a special consultant."

I looked at Blackhawk. He was smiling.

Jane Marie looked at Blackhawk. "I think I know you," she said.

Blackhawk looked surprised.

"How do you know him?" Mendoza said.

"Don't you tend bar in a joint down off 19th Avenue? Place with three bars in it."

"Part time," he said with a smile.

"Yeah, I've been in there. Really good salsa band."

Mendoza cleared his throat, "I think you deserve a complete explanation, if you'll do this. You can volunteer, but no one will order you to do it." He looked at her, waiting.

"Oh, I'm in," Jane Marie said, grinning. "How can I resist working with a guy named Blackhawk and get to cover my body with henna tattoos."

"Actually, that's a good idea," Boyce said.

Mendoza glanced at his watch. "Mr. Jackson and Mr.

Blackhawk are civilians. They have helped the department in the past. I have informed the commander as to what we plan to do, and he has agreed that we keep it in this room. In a bureaucracy, too many cooks can spoil the broth."

Funny, I'd just heard that somewhere.

"I'll need some technical help," Boyce said.

He nodded. He turned and nodded at me.

"Friends of mine," I said, "have identified a stripper in one of the organization's clubs who, we think, will want to take advantage of the thousand-dollar offer. Once we're ready to go, you and I will go in while she's working. I'll be a drunk who tries to pimp you out. You will just have to play along. We'll time it so that I get sick the same time she takes her break. If she doesn't come to you, you'll find a way to start talking to her. Maybe about getting a job there, whatever. If I'm right, she'll set you up with Julie Wang."

"That doesn't sound too hard," Jane Marie said.

"We will be nearby at all times," Boyce said.

"We'll keep you safe," Blackhawk said.

"I'm not worried," Jane Marie said.

"I doubt it will get rough, but it might," I said.

"I can get rough," Jane Marie said. "Just ask Melly Estevez."

"Who's that?" I said.

"The asswipe I busted two nights ago for dealing off his porch in my precinct."

"You had to get rough?" Boyce said.

"Twelve stitches behind his ear for resisting arrest. He put his hands on me, and I'm just like John Wayne. I won't be laid a hand on."

"And you won't be wronged, you won't be insulted, you don't do these things to other people and you require the same from them."

Jane Marie grinned. It made her look even younger.

"Okay," Mendoza said shaking his head. He looked at Jane Marie. "You are now assigned to Detective Boyce. I'll clear it with your commander. Now, get out of here, I'm busy."

We stood and started making our way out.

"This could be dangerous," Boyce said to Jane Marie.

"Cool," Jane Marie said.

51

The joint was called The Hi-Life Club. It was off of Camelback. Once in the door it was like every strip club in the world. Maybe a little dingier. Boyce and I had met Jane Marie at the Phoenix PD building downtown. She looked great. Hair was spiked and sprayed with blue streaks. She wore a small pair of cutoffs and a tube top. The wire was in her key chain which she carried in her pocket.

She had tattoos on one ankle and a larger one on the small of her back. One arm had a sleeve of tattoos, dragons and demons. I had Nacho give me a teardrop tattoo and he added some prison tats on my bicep and knuckles. I wore an Aerosmith tee shirt with the arms ripped off and blue jeans.

Before we got to the club I gargled some bourbon and spilled some down my shirt. I parked in the back of the lot. I paid the cover charge and we went in. I saw Nacho and Indigo in the far corner. I led Jane Marie to a table close enough to the front so the strippers could notice her. The room was dominated by a rectangle of extra wide bar, with poles on each corner. Each pole was busy, plus there were two other girls on the bar gyrating to throbbing music. I think it was music. Hard to tell.

Around the perimeter of the room were tables and chairs. They were mostly empty. One lap dance was going on. Across the room Nacho and Indigo sat at one of these. Most of the stools at the bar were filled with guys.

A waitress came to us immediately. This was a classier place. She wore a top. I ordered two beers and a shot. When she came with the drinks, I put up a twenty, held up a finger to hold her there, downed the shot and ordered another one.

Jane Marie pulled her phone from her back pocket and began fiddling with it. I looked across the room at Nacho. He was watching me. When he saw me looking, he looked toward the stripper closest to him. I looked at her. *Starbright.* When I looked back at him, he nodded.

The waitress came back with my shot. I handed her another twenty. She leaned down to speak to me above the din.

"You have already paid, sir. I have your change."

I waved her away. "Keep it."

Jane Marie looked at me and loudly said, "You're drunk!"

I downed the shot and drew my hand back, like I was going to hit her. She cowered back. I slammed the shot glass on the table and took a long drink of beer. I leaned back and looked at the girls. Jane Marie went back to her phone. The signal was, when Starbright took her break, Nacho would stand and go to the bathroom.

I immediately drank most of the beer. I kept ordering shots. I would toss the shot back, then take a drink of beer.

Except instead of drinking the beer I spit the shot into the beer bottle. I made it obvious that I was getting drunker by the drink. Jane Marie kept sliding her chair further from me. I could see the girls glancing at her.

Finally, the music broke, and Nacho stood and moved toward the back where the restrooms were. I stood and swayed against the table, then lost my balance and fell back, knocking a chair down. I sat down, hard. The bouncer was right there.

"Whoa, buddy. You've had enough."

The guy was a mass of muscle in a black tee shirt and motorcycle boots.

I held on to him. "I think I'm going to be sick," I mumbled.

"Not here, get to the restroom." He grabbed my arm and dragged me to the back. Holding the wall for support, I stumbled to the men's room. I pushed my way inside. Nacho was at a urinal. I pushed one of the two stall doors open and went in. God, only a pig would use this thing. I made retching noises as I pulled the wireless earpiece out of my pocket. I plugged it into my ear just as I heard a woman's voice say, "You gonna be okay, honey?"

Jane Marie's voice was tinny, but clear enough. Boyce and one of PD's techies were outside recording.

"Yeah," I heard her say. "He's just drunk. He gets that way."

"He your boyfriend?"

Oh, fuck no."

"Who is he?"

"I kinda work for him."

"He your pimp?"

Jane Marie was silent for a long pause. "I don't like that word. He's my handler."

"Yeah, like you're a fuckin' rock star. Why do you waste your time with a loser like that?"

Jane Marie didn't say anything, I'm guessing she shrugged.

"You make any money with this guy?" the girl said. I think Jane Marie shrugged again. She didn't say anything.

"You want to make some real money?" the girl said.

"Doin' what? Pole dancing?"

"Maybe, don't knock it. Sometimes I make five hundred a night. Sometimes we get to go to business parties and make a couple of thousand a night."

"Business parties?"

"Yeah, business parties. High rollers come from out of town and party up. Get away from the wife. Big money, big tippers. One time they flew some of us girls to Cancun on a private jet. It was a blast."

"Shit, I'd like to get some of that."

"Look, you're young and you're cute and that sells. You come back here tomorrow night at six, it opens at seven. You tell the door guy Starbright told you to come. He'll let you in. I'll hook you up."

There was a silence and then the music started again. I could barely hear Jane Marie. "Why would you do that?"

"None of us girls likes an asshole. We don't have to put up with them. Why should you? Come see me tomorrow."

I stuck the earpiece into my pocket. I went out of the stall and splashed water on my face. I made sure to soak the front of my shirt. I went back out. Jane Marie was sitting where I'd left her. She was watching the pole dancers. Nacho and Indigo were gone.

I went over and grabbed Jane Marie by the upper arm and jerked her out of her chair. "We're going," I said loudly. I bumped against the table and knocked my beer bottle over. She followed me out.

52

Boyce and I sat in a van a half block from the Hi-Life Club. Joining us was the PD techie that handled the recording equipment. His name was Stan. He was a big guy, not fit, just big. He looked to be in his forties, with a beard and bad teeth. I never understood bad teeth. Unless you're below the poverty line, there's no reason for it. I know this guy had health benefits with the city. He should use them.

He had Jane Marie on the speaker phone. We watched as she walked across the parking lot and disappeared into the club.

"Starbright asked me to come." We heard her voice. It was clear. Stan reached over and tweaked a couple of dials.

"She's in back," a male voice said. "Follow me."

We could hear some extraneous noises as they moved through the club. It took longer than you would think. We picked up some voices, then "Hey, there she is."

"Hi," Jane Marie said.

"I want you to meet someone," Starbright said. "This is Julie Wang. What did you say your name was, hon?"

"Cindy," Jane Marie said.

"Cindy what, dear?" this was another voice.

"Cindy Nowanski," she said.

"Oh my, we'll have to do something about that," Julie Wang said.

"I'm Starbright," Starbright said, "she can be Starlight."

Boyce and I looked at each other.

"No, too similar. We don't want the customers confused. You are a tiny little thing. I'll call you Belle as in Tinker Bell. Only with an 'e'."

"You can call me whatever you want but, uh, Starbright said we're talking lots of money. What I want to know is what kind of money, and what do I have to do to get it."

"You ever danced before?"

"No."

"We'll go out front, see how you do."

"I ain't never did it before," Jane Marie said.

"That's okay. Starbright says you've been tricking for some asshole."

There was silence. "That true?"

Silence again, then "I guess so," Jane Marie said. Just the right amount of hesitancy.

"You guess so? You fuck men for money or you don't fuck men for money. So do you, or don't you?"

"Yes," I could barely hear her.

"So what happens to the money?"

Jane Marie hesitated. "I give it to Jimmy."

"How much do you get?"

"Jimmy says I don't need much. He gives me a couple

hundred a week. He says he gives me more than that, I'll just stick it in my arm."

"You do drugs?"

"No."

"Then why'd he say that?"

"Cause that's what he does. I don't do drugs."

"Let me see your arms." There was some extraneous noise.

"I can put you to work, you can make two thousand a week to start. What'd you think of that?"

"I don't want to fuck just anybody. I'm clean, I got no STDs and I want to stay that way."

"All of our clients are respectable. I want you to be clean for them. Last thing we want is to get a bad reputation. We'll have you examined. So, you ready to go to work?"

"I got to fuck somebody today?"

"Eventually, but no, not today. We have some work to do on you first."

"What kind of work?"

"We have to do something about your hair and get you a wardrobe. But now, let's go see if you can dance."

We listened to the rustling as they moved back into the bar.

"Get up on that pole, let's see what you can do." Julie Wangs voices was farther away, echoing in the empty room. There was more rustling.

"There ain't no music," Jane Marie said.

"Just dance," Julie Wangs voice was even farther away. "The customers don't give a damn about the music."

Now there was some rustling. We could hear Jane Marie's breath become harder with exertion.

Finally, Julie Wang said, "Stop. God girl, you can't dance worth a shit."

"I'm sorry. I'm trying," Jane Marie said.

"That's okay," Julie Wang said. She was closer now. "I'm not hiring you to dance, anyway. How old are you?"

"Twenty-one."

"She looks fifteen," Starbright said.

"Yeah, she'll be real popular. You have a phone?"

"Don't everybody have a phone?"

"And we're going to have to do something about the way you talk."

"What's wrong with the way I talk?" Jane Marie said, sounding offended.

"You don't sound educated. *Don't* everybody have a phone. It should be *doesn't* everybody have a phone. I need you to be able to talk to important men. They don't want to screw some cracker."

"Probably won't matter with her, young as she is," Starbright said.

"Yeah probably, but I don't like it anyway. Give me your phone number."

Jane Marie gave it to her.

"Now, give me your phone." It was a burner Boyce had supplied.

More rustling. A long moment with nothing.

Finally, Julie Wang said, "Here, I put my number in it. You don't call me. If you do it better be important. Don't call me anywhere but that number. Don't call the club, don't call anywhere but that number. If I don't answer I will call you back. Got it?"

"Yes."

"And, from now on you call me ma'am. You understand?"

"Yes, ma'am."

"Okay, I will text you the doctors name, address and appointment time. I will text you the salon I want you to go to and the time. Once your hairs right, we'll get you a wardrobe. Got it?"

"Yes ma'am."

More rustling. Julie Wang said, "Here's five hundred dollars. Don't go back to Jimmy the asshole. Don't go back to where you live and get anything. Go to the mall and get everything you need. Get a new place to live. Here's a card for a realtor. Call her, tell her you work for me and have her get you a furnished weekly rental. You won't need cash. I will be in touch in two days. Go to this doctor today. We have a party to go to, day after tomorrow. My boss will be in town. He is having an event at his place in Paradise Valley. There will be a lot of important people there. Congressmen, dignitaries, that kind of thing. We want you looking good because you are just his type. I know he would want to meet you. But you have to look a lot better. Welcome aboard, now get out of here."

A few minutes later Jane Marie came out of the building, went to her car and drove away.

53

Blackhawk and I were sitting in his office. It was after midnight and the band was done. He had been unusually quiet. We were both enjoying a Ballantine's on the rocks. The room had been soundproofed so we could just hear our own breathing.

He looked at me. "You know I'm going to take this guy."

"Hesse?"

"Yeah, Hesse. This asshole is mine. Nobody takes Elena and makes it out alive."

"We took care of Luis."

He shook his head. "Luis wasn't the head of the snake. This guy is the head of the snake."

"Mendoza is going to lock him up."

"I don't know if that's good enough. He'll still be around breathing."

"You kill the guy and Mendoza may lock you up."

He looked at his drink and was silent.

"It's too late to start another action. We've already got this with Jane Marie going. We have to see it through."

"I want him dead."

I looked at him for a long time. He wouldn't look at me. Finally, I said, "What would Elena want you to do?"

Still staring at his drink, he slowly began to smile. "You sneaky son of a bitch," he said. He looked at me. "You know just what to stick in me."

At eleven the next morning Blackhawk and I met Boyce and Jane Marie in front of the downtown PD headquarters. Jane Marie was in her uniform. Boyce nodded without saying anything. She turned and started into the building. We followed. She led the way to an interrogation room. She stopped and looked at Blackhawk and me. She indicated another door.

"You guys can watch from in there. You'll be able to see and hear everything. There's a speaker on the wall. The on/off switch is underneath."

She opened the door and I followed Blackhawk in. To our right was a two-way mirror. The speaker was next to it. Blackhawk switched it on. On the other side Julie Wang sat with her lawyer. She was in handcuffs. A policeman stood in the corner. We had a wait. Finally, the door opened, and Boyce and Officer Landers came in. They were followed by Mendoza and another suit.

The speaker had a faint hum to it. Mendoza said, "If you'll wait outside, officer."

The policeman left. There were enough chairs for everyone. They all sat.

Mendoza looked from Julie Wang to her lawyer. "I am Captain Mendoza of the Phoenix Police Department," he said. "This is Mr. Walker, of the State's Attorney's office." He didn't introduce Boyce or Jane Marie. "And you are?" he said to Wang's attorney.

"I represent Miss Wang. My name is John Mahan."

"Good," Mendoza said. "Mr. Walker has a proposal for you. But first you both need to hear this." He pulled a device from his pocket and set it on the table. He pushed a button. It was tinny, but we heard Julie Wang's voice.

"That's okay. Starbright says you've been tricking for some asshole."

There was silence. "That true?"

Silence again, then "I guess so" Jane Marie said.

"You guess so? You fuck men for money or you don't fuck men for money. So, do you, or don't you?"

"Yes."

"So, what happens to the money?"

Jane Marie, "I give it to Jimmy."

"How much do you get?"

"Jimmy says I don't need much. He gives me a couple hundred a week. He says he gives me more than that, I'll just stick it in my arm."

"You do drugs?"

"No."

"Then why'd he say that?"

"Cause that's what he does. I don't do drugs."

"Let me see your arms."

"I can put you to work, you can make two thousand a week. What'd you think of that."

"I don't want to fuck just anybody. I'm clean, I got no STD's and I want to stay that way."

"All of our clients are respectable. I want you to be clean for them. Last thing we want is to get a bad reputation. We'll have you examined. So, you ready to go to work?"

"I got to fuck somebody today?"

"Eventually, but no, not today. We have some work to do on you first."

Mendoza reached over and shut it off. Julie Wang had paled.

The attorney said, "This is inadmissible."

Mr. Walker said, "We had a warrant. Miss Wang, we can put you into Florence for a long, long time. Or you can cooperate with us."

Julie Wang was looking at the table. She raised her eyes and looked at Jane Marie like she was seeing her for the first time. "What do you want?"

"We want William S. Hesse. If you help us, we can offer substantially reduced charges."

"I need to talk with my attorney."

Mendoza stood. The others followed.

"Of course," Mr. Walker said.

Mendoza said, "Detective Boyce, if you would escort Mr. Mahan and Miss Wang to the anteroom 2B where they can have a private conversation." He nodded at Officer Jane Marie Landers and Jane Marie opened the door. They all filed out, Boyce following Julie Wang and her attorney.

A moment later our door opened, and Mendoza came in. I waited. I knew what was coming. He didn't disappoint.

"Did you hear all that okay?"

I nodded.

"Okay, then. We appreciated your help and initiative, we can take it from here."

"What's the plan?" Blackhawk said.

Mendoza looked at him. "If Hesse is in town tomorrow, as Miss Wang has said. we'll send Miss Wang and Officer Landers in to see him. We'll get him on tape. We'll throw his ass in jail."

"I want to be there," Blackhawk said.

Mendoza looked at him. "What's your stake in this?"

"Nikki Boyd and Simone Dove," he said.

"Emily Sykes," I said.

"Friends of yours?"

"Elena befriended them."

Mendoza looked puzzled. "Elena hanging out with prostitutes?"

"Elena loves all animals, large and small," Blackhawk said. "Even broken soiled doves."

"We'll stay out of the way. We just want to watch it go down," I said.

Mendoza was quiet for a long moment. "You can stay in the surveillance truck. You stay out of the way." He gave me a hard look. If we weren't such close chums, I might have been intimidated.

54

One of Hesse's corporations had been renting an estate in Paradise Valley. It was close to the Phoenician Resort off of Invergordon. It was walled and gated. It had ten bedrooms. It looked like it could be a resort by itself. Blackhawk and I had looked at the architectural schematics the night before.

The sun was low in the sky and the guests had begun to arrive. There were two men at the gate checking invitations. There was valet parking at the front foyer with an empty lot across the street acting as the parking lot. There was a man at the door, opening it for the guests. Julie Wang had said there were usually four or five others armed, working as waiters.

Stan, Stan the audio man, was inside the van with Boyce and me. I could smell him. Boyce had given Blackhawk and me an ear bud. Blackhawk had taken his to the passenger seat of the van. It was too crowded in the back. We had been listening to silence. Julie Wang and Jane Marie were with SWAT. They had Julie's car so they could drive up to the valet. They were wired but weren't talking. I think Julie was miffed.

There were two SWAT teams, each one on opposite sides, two blocks away and ready to roll. The SWAT commander was named Henderson and it would be his to call. He needed to hear enough to indict Hesse. In the meantime, Jane Marie would be in jeopardy.

Boyce and I tried to be as comfortable as possible, watching the screens. She was amusing herself by telling me who the dignitaries were as they arrived. There were athletes and congressmen, and business leaders. I don't know what I expected. I guess I thought it would be a stag party, but it wasn't. Most of the men had a female date. Boyce named a baseball player I'd never heard of, but that was no mean feat. I don't really follow baseball.

"What? You subscribe to People magazine?" I said. "How do you know who these people are?"

"I'm a trained detective," she said. She leaned forward looking at a screen. "There they are," she said.

Sure enough, a Porsche 911 pulled up through the gates. It was waved forward, and the valet jumped forward to open the driver's door, then raced around to open the passenger door. Julie Wang stepped out of the driver's seat. Jane Marie came out the other. Jane Marie had lost the blue highlights in her hair. She was dressed in a simple black dress and high heels. She had a plain strand of dime store pearls around her neck, and a gawdy looking piece of costume jewelry on her wrist. The wire was in the bracelet. Julie Wang wore a short dress that almost covered her. Over the top was a draped chiffon thing that went to her knees but was completely transparent. She carried a small cocktail purse. Her wire was in the lining of the purse. I could hear the rustling of both as they stepped out of the $200,000 Porsche. I thought crime wasn't supposed to pay.

Julie Wang handed the keys to the valet and they went up the steps. I heard her say, "Hello Gary," to the guy opening the door. "Good evening Miss Wang," Gary said. They disappeared inside. I could hear music and indistinguishable chatter.

"Follow me," I heard Julie Wang say. More noise. After a very long time I heard a door close and the background noise went away. They had gone into a room and shut the door.

"Is this the young lady you told me about?" a male voice.

"Yes. This is Belle. Belle, this is our boss, Mr. Hesse."

"May I fix you girls a drink," Hesse said.

"Gin and tonic," Julie Wang said.

There was a clinking of bottles. "How about you Belle, what can I fix you?"

"A beer, I guess," Jane Marie said.

"I'm afraid I don't have beer. Never cared for it myself. How about a gin and tonic like Julie's?"

"Sure."

"She is very young looking," he said.

"Yes," Julie Wang said. "I thought you might want to see this one."

More soft clinking noises. "Here you are, dear."

"Thanks," Jane Marie said.

"How old are you, dear?"

"Twenty-one."

"She looks twelve," he said.

"Yes, she does," Julie Wang said. "I don't think I want to put her in a club. I think she'll be more valuable for specialty customers."

"I can see that." Silence, then, "Belle, has Miss Wang explained what you will be doing for us, and how much money you can make?"

"Well, uh...., she said you'd be setting me up on dates and I'd probably end up having to fuck them, but they'd pay a whole lot of money to do it."

I could hear him laugh. "Crudely put, but basically accurate." I heard the clinking of glass again. "You aren't drinking your drink. Drink up. Go ahead, drink up, I'll make another."

We could hear Jane Marie swallow. The mic in the bracelet was right next to her mouth.

"Good girl. Here, give me your glass."

More glass clinking. "Julie, why don't you leave us alone for a moment."

"I'll see to the guests," Julie Wang said.

A moment more and we heard the door close. There was noise from Julie Wang's mic.

"Shut her back," Boyce said to Stan.

He fiddled with a knob and the crowd noise diminished.

"Drink your drink, dear," Hesse said.

Again, the drinking sound.

"What are you doing?" Jane Marie said.

"I don't buy something without testing the merchandise," Hesse said. "Let's take that dress off, dear."

"Don't," Jane Marie said loudly. There were scuffling noises.

"Don't," Jane Marie screamed. There was the sound of flesh hitting flesh.

"You little bitch." More scuffling and more blows landed.

"We're going in." Henderson's voice was in my ear.

Then Boyce said, "Where is he going?" On the screen, Blackhawk was rapidly walking toward the two guards standing in the driveway.

55

I went out the back of the van and started hotfooting it after Blackhawk. Can a guy with only one-foot *hotfoot it*? The thing about Blackhawk is that even in his everyday attire, he still looked like he belonged at the party.

The two guys saw him coming but had no idea why. They converged on him, presumably to ask for his ticket when Blackhawk kicked the first guy in the knee. The guy went down and the other guy reached under his coat and Blackhawk punched him in the throat. The guy staggered back. He had managed to pull his pistol. Blackhawk took it and slapped him in the temple with it. The guy went down.

The first guy had rolled to his side holding his knee, but now realized what was happening. He reached for his pistol. Blackhawk backhanded him with the other guy's pistol. The guy went face down. There were a few people standing around. They were gawking at Blackhawk, but no one made a move.

The guard at the door drew his pistol and started down the steps, pointing it at Blackhawk. Blackhawk shot him in the forehead. Anyone else would aim for center mass. Not the wild man, he shoots them in the forehead. He ran to the door and went inside. I was moving, seconds behind him. Behind me I could hear Boyce yelling my name. Yelling for me to stop. Yeah right.

I heard gunfire inside. I went in fast, angling to the right, my Kahr in my hand. People were screaming and rushing the door in a panic to get out. A man lay on the stairs holding his thigh. Blood ran between his fingers. A pistol lay on the floor below him. Blackhawk was at the top of the stairs, grappling with a guy that had grabbed him. He looked like a civilian. Trying to be a hero. Bad move. He was tall and rangy and tried to wrap Blackhawk up in a bear hug. Blackhawk kneed the guy in the groin and he leaned forward, his face distorted in pain. Blackhawk pushed him aside. The upstairs had closed doors. We had choices. The master bedroom was the second door to the right. What's behind door number two. Blackhawk found out by opening it and walking in. I went by the civilian holding his groin and was right behind.

William S. Hesse was sitting, sprawled on the floor, back against the bed. He had his hand to his mouth, which was bleeding badly. Officer Jane Marie Landers was standing over him with a mark over her eye that would be a dandy shiner tomorrow. In her hand was an iron bookend. When Blackhawk had come in, she had spun, ready to throw the bookend at him. The shoulder strap on her little black dress was broken. There was a scratch across her throat and shoulder.

Boyce followed me in. She walked over to Jane Marie. "You okay?"

Jane Marie nodded.

Boyce turned to us. "Give me your weapons." She held her hand out. Blackhawk didn't move, and I didn't know if he was going to comply. I handed her mine.

"SWAT is coming up the stairs. Give me your weapon," she said again.

Blackhawk handed it to her. She tossed the pistols on the bed, and SWAT burst into the room.

"Put your hands on your head!" they were screaming. "Put your hands on your head." Blackhawk and I complied. Boyce ignored them. They grabbed us roughly and pushed us against the wall. They cuffed us both.

Boyce watched this calmly. I think she liked it. She reached to her back pocket and pulled a badge. She tossed it to Jane Marie, who caught it deftly with one hand.

"This belongs to you. This guy is yours, you do the honors," Boyce said.

Jane Marie squatted down to Hesse's eye level. She held the badge in front of him. "Okay, ass wipe. You are under arrest for a number of things, not the least of which is assaulting a police officer. Other charges will be outlined for you downtown. In the meantime, you have the right to remain silent. You have the right to an attorney." She read him his rights.

When she finished, Boyce handed her some cuffs and Jane Marie snapped them on one wrist. She deftly turned him onto his stomach, put her knee in his back and cuffed the other one. He was bleeding all over his nice carpeting. In the meantime, I was being frisked. Not gently.

56

It was Labor Day and the marina was a giant, festering party. Everyone in Phoenix had gone to the lake. It was warm, but a strong breeze came from the west, so in the shade it was not unpleasant. No pun intended. Get it? Lake Pleasant, unpleasant? Never mind.

The way we had decided to protect ourselves from all the interlopers was to gather on Pete's boat with heavily stocked coolers, a full bar and good friends. Red meat was in Pete's locker and the charcoal grill was banked, ready for the match. Blackhawk and Elena were working. In the night club business, you took advantage of every holiday.

However, Lindy and Ashley had joined us, along with Eddie, Captain Rand and some of his friends. Some I had met, some I hadn't. My goal was to get a small, non-invasive but effective buzz going, and maintain it as long as possible.

Lindy had brought a fella she had met at Ashley's school. He had a daughter in Ashley's class and was a single parent also. The two girls were decked out in life jackets and, with prolonged shrieks, were jumping off of Pete's stern, climbing back up the ladder and doing it again. They had been at it for two hours. Lindy and her friend were nursing Coronas, sitting under the over-hang watching the girls. I was pretty sure that at least one of them was also watching the bikinied young things that were draped over the ski boats that putted by.

Pete was heavily involved in a backgammon game with one of Captain Rand's young lady friends. Two guys and their wives were at the galley table playing poker. The women were pretending to not know how to play, but earlier, when I went to the head, I noticed they had the chips. Eddie, Captain Rand and I were content to snuggle into Pete's deck chairs on the bow and watch the world go by.

When Lindy and Ashley had arrived, Ashley took great delight in explaining to her friend that I had been the poopy head three times running. This meant I had to explain to Lindy's friend how you played poopy head. Ashley insisted we do it before they could leave.

As the sun began its dive behind the far blue mountains, Pete fired the grill and I helped in the galley. We served up everything on the galley counter and we ate like kings. The kids topped it off with bowls of ice cream, and that about did them in.

Unfortunately, my ambitions to be poopy head four times running were thwarted by time getting by. Lindy firmly explained it was a school night and they took their leave as the sun was down.

Slowly, one by one and couple by couple, the group began to dissipate until finally it was Captain Rand, Eddie,

Pete and me up top watching the stars come out. Pete brought a bottle of Glenlivet and a bowl of ice up and we sipped it in that way when you take just enough into the mouth and let it saturate your whole body. You swallow slowly, and sometimes smack your lips and you close your eyes and look inward. When the Glenlivet showed up the conversation tailed off. We sat in mellowed contemplation.

I was trying to rouse myself enough to take my leave, when we heard someone on the dock. Pete struggled his way out of his chair and went to the bow to look.

He came back. He looked at me. "Couple of friends," he said.

I pulled myself up and went to look. Blackhawk and Nacho came walking up. Blackhawk looked up at me, and then looked at the glass in my hand.

"You got more of that?"

"If Pete doesn't, I do," I said.

They joined us. Pete, the consummate host, pulled chaise lounge chairs for them and fixed them each a drink. Once they settled, Pete raised his glass and we all toasted.

"One thing you haven't told me," Pete said. We all looked at him. "How come you guys aren't in jail?" He looked at Blackhawk. "You shot that guy right in front of God, cops and everybody."

Blackhawk looked at his drink.

"They took us downtown," I said. "But after Detective Boyce and Mendoza had the DA look at the video, they could see the guy on the porch clearly point a weapon at Blackhawk before Blackhawk shot him." I shrugged. "Self-defense. And it didn't hurt there was a cop upstairs being assaulted."

"So," Pete said, "would you still have shot him if he hadn't pointed his gun at you?"

Blackhawk was still looking at his drink. I looked at mine.

"When I bought this boat," Pete said, "I thought it was going to be all peace and quiet and secluded. Next time I'll vet the neighbors a little better."

"Ain't this a lot more fun," Eddie said.

I raised my glass.

After a while, Blackhawk looked at me. "Indigo left," he said.

"Left?"

"The colonel," he said. That was all he had to say.

Nacho looked at me. "She said once she wanted to see New York City. This colonel guy is he in New York?"

I shook my head. Finally, I said, "You okay?"

"Oh, hell yeah," he said. "I liked her, a lot, but she could have an edge to her. And she wore me out."

"Ain't met a woman yet that couldn't do that," Captain Rand said.

Blackhawk put his mouth into his glass to get the best reverb. "They called her Indigo," he said in his movie trailer voice.

"Now they call her Indigone," Nacho said.

Following is an excerpt from
number five in the acclaimed Jackson Blackhawk series.
Coming Soon

THE DARKER HOURS

a Detective Boyce mystery

by Sam Lee Jackson

THE DARKER HOURS

Boyce was dreaming. In one of those places where you are eighty percent asleep, but aware of the other twenty. She was irritated because Jackson was in the dream. They were trying to fit bolts on the bottom of something and the bolts wouldn't thread right. And then Jackson was grinning at her and making a weird noise, and it pissed her off.

She said, "Shut up Jackson," and woke up. Her phone was buzzing. She looked at the clock. It was three thirty-four in the morning. She slid over to the side and sat up. She picked up her phone. She was a Detective of the Phoenix police department and you answer the phone.

"Boyce," she said.

"Detective, sorry to bother you at this hour," she recognized the voice of Lieutenant Hicks. He was the late show watch commander.

"Yes, sir," she said, resisting the urge to tell him she had to get up to answer the phone anyway.

"We have a situation here that, I think, needs your attention."

"A situation?"

"A homicide."

"I thought Grennel was on duty, I'm assigned to gangs."

"He is. He's here, but I think you need to come down. I know, you have fifty questions. I don't want to get into them on the phone. I'd just like for you to come down."

"Yes, sir," she said. "Give me the address."

He did.

It took her a half an hour.

The location was a quiet residential neighborhood west of 32nd Street and north of Shea Boulevard. A normal neighborhood. Close to the high school, moderately priced homes, safe, secure, a family place. People here had kids that went to that school. There were block watches, PTA meetings. A great neighborhood to trick or treat. Now full of black and whites, with lights flashing eerily against the modest ranch style homes, with the street blocked off.

Boyce pulled up to the black and white and flashed her badge at the patrol officer blocking the street. He waved her through and she pulled up as near as she could to the PPD Homicide wagon. She pulled cross-wise in a drive way and got out. She knew the civilian who owned the driveway would be screaming about having to go to work in about an hour. She hoped she wouldn't be here that long.

There were teenagers and parents huddled in groups. Strangely quiet. Some were crying. Two ambulances were being loaded by EMTs. These kids were the lucky ones. There were two not-so-lucky on the front lawn, covered by army green tarps. Hicks was standing next to one of them.

She walked over to him.

She took her time. She looked all around. Looking at nothing and looking at everything. She noted a bullet starred window behind the bodies. Chunks of plaster dug out of the stucco. The home was just as ordinary looking as the others. Common for this neighborhood. Hicks was making notes on his phone. The crime scene team were taking pictures. When Boyce reached him, Hicks held a finger up to ward her off while he finished his notes.

She waited.

Finally, he put the phone away. He pulled another phone from his jacket. It had one of those cases that holds your credit card and your driver's license, so you don't have a lot of baggage. He slipped his finger in the sleeve and worked a folded photograph out. He unfolded it and handed it to Boyce.

There were two women in the photo. She was one of them. They were in a potato sack race and laughing hysterically.

"Oh shit," Boyce said. She squatted down and slipped the tarp back. The girl was seventeen. Dark hair, a real beauty. Her torso was soaked with dark blood. She was face down, her face turned slightly. A strand of her hair was across her face. She wore a striped green top with no sleeves and faded maroon shorts. One foot still had a flip-flop on it. The other was bare.

Boyce stayed beside the girl for a very long time. Using one finger, she moved the hair off the girl's face. She finally stood.

She looked at Hicks. He was watching her.

"You know who this is?" Boyce asked him.

"I know what her driver's license says, but no, I don't," he said. "But, it appears you do. That's why I called."

Boyce took a long breath and let it out, ever so slowly. "Her name is Olivia Cromwell."

"She related?"

Boyce shook her head. "Not by blood. But she's family. Livvy is the eldest daughter of Dorotea Cromwell." Boyce looked at Henderson. "Dorotea is Captain Mendoza's youngest sister."

"Well, shit," Henderson said.

Did you enjoy
They Called Her Indigo?

If you enjoyed this book, please go online to where you bought it and let us know what you think. After you get there, just click on the book you read, then click on the reviews. Thanks for reading.

Go online to the address below to leave a review, or for more Jackson Blackhawk reading adventures

www.samleejackson.com